June 2, 2021

Hi Carolyn,

Enjoy this
Review
Copy!
Thanks, so much!

Julianny

RIPPLES

A NOVEL

JULIANNE BIEN

A SPECTRAHUE PUBLICATION

STORIES BY BIEN

Color: Awakening the Child Within

Adventures of Maximojo: A Warp in Time

Zeetumah: Queen of the Rainbow Honeybees

Copyright © 2021 Julianne Bien

Published by Spectrahue Light & Sound Inc.,
PO Box 38156 RPO Castlewood, Toronto, ON, Canada M5N 3A9
spectrahue.com

Bien, Julianne
Title: Ripples / Julianne Bien.
First Edition 2021

ISBN: 978-1-987956-08-5 (paperback)
ISBN: 978-1-987956-09-2 (ebook)

Printed and bound in Canada

Cover design & layout:
Julianne Bien

Cover photos courtesy of:
Award-winning, steel-sculptor Daniella Boerhof, Ontario, Canada

DEDICATED TO MY GRANDMOTHER PEARL

(1911-1980 Gemini)

CONTENT

- CHAPTER 1 -
Toronto, April 2022

I know about fate. There's no escaping it.

The bronze skeleton key fit into the heavy iron lock, and the door bolted shut. I replaced the key in its box under the porch bench, officially ending my midnight shift.

The log cabin was originally a trading post, built nearly two and a half centuries ago, close to the city docks. With the construction and development that had occurred over the last two centuries, it was now nearly a mile inland as if stranded on the edge of the downtown by the passage of time.

The all-night Khilto's Metaphysical Bookstore & Café was closed for the next few hours—all night does not include the time from 7 AM to noon. Brass doorbell chimes announced the usual customers at their usual times. Its lingering resonance kept unwanted spirits away. Khilto's was a favorite place for insomniac booklovers to while away the moonlit hours.

Well-versed literary patrons would browse the shelves and sit down at vintage school desks, complete with dried-up inkwells and penknife graffiti declaring puppy love, while preserving the memories of schoolchildren long since become grandparents or passed on.

There was a special selection called Khilto's bedtime library, for nightly regulars. They could store their favorite books in the desks' lift-up lids, paying for their use of the space and reading materials through hourly coffee and muffin purchases. I would watch them forgetting their cares, cradling a book like a newborn when a well-crafted line of prose struck a heart cord.

The building is a city landmark. The name Khilto is carved on a broken wood plank over the entrance door. Urban legend has it that it came from a shipwreck that had washed ashore nearby. An old 19th-century potbelly iron stove is our cozy fireplace in the reading room. Stories were told about the early settlement wards around it.

A brass plaque on the door gave a brief history of the site: originally a soldier's bunkhouse, its basements became a gunpowder magazine in the War of 1812. Later, when peace fell across the American border, it became an ordinary warehouse, which it remained until the progressive filling of the lakeshore and increasing size of ships moved the real dockyards away from that part of Toronto.

It served over the following years as a place of various types, until Hurricane Hazel flooded its basements in 1954. Abandoned for several years, it was saved from demolition when a film producer saw a potential set for a historical romance. He sealed off the ruined cellars and fixed the rest of the building. When the film was done, he sold it to the current owner, who made it into a bookstore and coffee shop.

We always kept a stash of marshmallows to roast on toasting sticks. The coffee counter, standing near a trapdoor, is a vintage piece found at the roadside during a library demolition. I stand there all night, or at the muffin oven, and I wear home the shop's aroma of fresh roasted beans.

Metaphysical, new age, classics and antiquarian books lined the shelves. We also have serious contemporary fiction for the literary critics who eye the selection in our window display, and fantasy and science fiction for those seeking escape. The thirst for the printed word brings them in, and they stay for my muffins and coffee. Whether a small latte or an extra-large cappuccino, I inscribe hieroglyphs in the almond milk froth, sprinkling it with cocoa, cinnamon, nutmeg or cardamom dust.

Rare antique map posters and prints of Toronto's history was chronological displayed along the walls. Like-minded people seek friendships under our slate shingle roof. Well-behaved small animals in tote bags are welcome too. I enjoy the weekend midnight shift. I would arrive around 10 PM, and usher out the last customer at daybreak, clean the dishes and empty the trashcans, then lock up at 7 AM. Khilto's owner would open the doors at noon, taking the longer and busier afternoon and evening shift.

Five past seven. It was a cool spring morning only a couple of decades into the 21st century. I couldn't wait to get home for a quick catnap. I had plans to meet Tom for brunch. I first saw him while roasting marshmallows during my shift last autumn, and my heart somersaulted in my chest. His laughing face of chiseled features framed with silver-flecked hair made his unusual blue eyes, mesmeric.

Tom's choice of reading material—more eclectic than most of our customers—also piqued my curiosity. He never ceases to surprise me with unexpected moments and curiosities. We were destined to meet each other.

I can still feel his lips on mine....

A pasty layer of dirty sand, clay and slit, still wet from snowmelt, covered the path that took me through a parking lot past a deep excavation to the main street. Another massive glass office tower would be going in here, the downtown creeping inexorably into what used to be a low-rise brick and stone neighborhood.

With a heavy tote slung over my shoulder, I angled my shoe on the curb to scrape off the muck that was ubiquitous at this time of year. I eyed the idle bulldozers and crane. My ankle throbbed from the metal plate and screws in my right foot as I stepped onto the sidewalk. A stoplight in the distance flickered from yellow to red.

Home was a third-floor walkup in a narrow building on a dead-end street, a block beyond that stoplight.

It was a converted five-story clothing factory from the 1920s. The sleek linear structure with geometric motifs, and a gentrified freight elevator carried an aura of Toronto's Art Deco history that even the uninitiated could sense. This had led to its designation as a heritage building.

The breaking dawn was warming the morning air. The wind rustled past me, spinning fresh litter and last year's dead leaves down the tree-lined, dimly lit street. As often happened after my midnight shift, I was daydreaming and listening to music.

Water droplets fell from the still bare branches. They plastered stray hairs to my forehead. I tucked the few unruly strands of my auburn hair around my ear for better music reception. The scent of coffee and musty books that my hair and hand-knit sweater had smuggled from the store, tickled my nostrils.

The crisp morning air was revitalizing. An iridescent halo over the dark watery clouds struck me as odd, with the sky's vivid otherworldly colors, etched across it. My hearing aid registered a crackling static sound over the retro folk rhythm guitar that was playing on my phone.

A whisper reverberated through the noise: "Iris. It is time." A wide-eyed face flashed faintly before me as her spoken words rippled down to my toes. I became acutely aware of the amulet that hung across my chest. My racing heart calmed down as my hands cradled the ancient relic with an instinctive urge to touch it.

I whirled around to face a deserted street.

I had a vision of a lost woman in a tunnel, calling me. Calling my name, Iris.

In my circle of friends, people only knew me as Irene, Irene Montgomery. But my given name at birth was Iris, and that's the name I had heard in the static. I believe supernatural phenomena doesn't abide by the law of Nature, but does exist everywhere, if we're able to perceive it. That is to say, tune into their presence. But the unexpected reality of possessing this ability has become increasingly apparent since my accident.

Without a second thought, my analytical mind took charge of this situation: I assured myself that I had not heard my name or saw anything, that it was just my imagination in the whistling wind. Or, maybe my hearing aid that doubled as a music ear bud was in need of a new battery. But there was a feeling of unreality to this morning. My mind drifted into what had transpired with Tom and this amulet, only twelve hours earlier....

It wasn't an ordinary afternoon before my midnight shift. Tom arrived just after one o'clock as we had planned. Barely in the foyer, Tom pulled me up against his chest as his hand guided my mouth to meet his. I was lost in his desire for me with his passionate, hungry kisses.

Tom swept my hair aside as my head drifted over for more. His seductive caress aroused the old Irene in me. Enveloped in his strong embrace, I felt his heat rise and my fingers fumbled to loosen his belt buckle. He slipped out of his jacket and shoes ... I unbuttoned his shirt.

My breath quickened with his curious touch under my sweatshirt. He swooped me up. We only made it as far as the kitchen where we indulged in pleasure until it was close to sunset. In utter bliss, with our bodies entwined lovingly, I kissed his lips and cheek lightly, giving him our signal. We squeezed into the shower stall laughing playfully. We lathered each other up, and talked about silly things.

Both dressed and ravenously hungry, I raided the refrigerator for Wednesday's leftover Chinese food. Tom leaned up against the kitchen counter satisfied with my homemade bittersweet chocolate-cherry biscotti, and a glass of fresh-squeezed orange juice.

In between mouthfuls, Tom told me matter-of-factly that during the winter cleanup of his aunt Margie's antique store, shortly after she got possession of it, he unearthed a vintage Ouija board. It was buried under a pile of junk below the basement stairwell.

"I'll show you, close your eyes...." Tom teased in a seductive voice as his body swung swiftly around me. With his hands nestled in the curve of my waist, I played along and my eyelids lowered. Tom inched me toward the front door. Step-by-step his burrowing butterfly kisses tickled the nape of my neck as I burst into giggles. I felt the breeze of his arm reach around me. My eyes opened with surprise. Tom had pulled out a wooden board from an oversized canvas bag. It was propped up beside his laptop on the floor.

When Tom arrived earlier on, I was unaware that he had placed it down. I hadn't seen him for a few days, and was swept away by an intense thirst for closeness. I wrapped my arms around his neck, with a kiss of gratitude for his animated gesture. Then I stepped back to observe the board. A warranted unease washed over me, and with it a warning signal.

"I've never seen anything like it, Irene. It's stunning, isn't it? Just look at the engraving along the outside edge, and all this beautiful mother-of-pearl and rosewood inlay. It must have belonged to someone wealthy. Margie's expert opinion assured me it speaks of 19th-century craftsmanship, with its exquisite detailing."

"It's a stunning piece, but, it is a Ouija board."

"Margie insisted that I take it home. When I showed it to her, she said it was meant for me as it didn't allow anyone else to find it. She has this intuitive knack of knowing. Sixth-sense stuff. Let's have some fun with it."

"How is your aunt's antique store doing?" I tried to change the subject.

"Margie only bought it last fall, and she has surpassed all expectations. It's booming even in this economy. By cleaning the place up from the previous owner's neglect, made a huge difference. She's grateful that you joined her on the inspection. You have incredible knowledge with these things. Margie values your opinion."

Tom placed the Ouija board down on the coffee table. It looked innocent enough, maybe nine inches by fourteen and hopefully harmless. With a far-away look in his eyes that was vague and eerily persistent. He pulled out an amulet from his jacket pocket that was hanging on the vintage coat stand in the front foyer.

My stomach stirred with a giddy sensation as he placed it in my hand. I was whisked excitedly away into another dimension. I thumbed the bronze and stone artifact: a sun-face set with rounded polished crystals at the cardinal points. An engraved script ran around the outer edge. The relic hung from a bronze chain that dangled down over my wrist. Baster's eyes followed its slow pendulum moves.

"You're the expert in ancient artifacts. Tell me its mysterious secret." Overcome with heightened sensitivity, my fingertips tingled with anticipation.

"My professional, anthropological opinion?" I studied the amulet intently. "It's certainly an unusual piece. It may be a lost family heirloom. Hmm, nice weight to it, too. I once read that a round pendant might hold a deity's spirit. This face is incredibly realistic. Its features have depth with human expression, and her mouth looks like its about to speak."

I turned on the magnifying glass on my phone. My fingers widened the image on the screen. "OMG! The crystal above her brow has a faint aura. Tom, do you see a faint hue around this stone? Check out this angle. See? It's a powder blue."

"Ah-ha! Do you think the amulet is some sort of radioactive device from a long-lost high civilization?

Maybe from Atlantis? Or, perhaps an alien artifact? Its glitter certainly catches your eye."

"Why not? Anything is possible in this world. Throughout the ages and in all cultures, people shielded themselves from evil spirits by encasing protective spiritual energies in hardened materials, such as statues or relics, and binding them with spells, incantations and rituals—even a simple prayer or a wish would do."

"Serious? So, if you break the amulet apart, a supernatural force will be unleashed? Good or bad?" Tom was lying on his side on the couch, knees bent and his arm angled upward. With chin in palm, he strummed his cheek. His eyes sparkled with enthusiasm. "Convince me, my sweet ghost-charmer!"

To play along I managed a silly curtsy. My fingers curled up over the amulet. I steady my mind to contemplate upon the object of its authenticity, and perhaps it origin. Fascinated, I dismissed the warm sensation that moved up my arm as my index finger skimmed along the hieroglyphs. The character symbols felt familiar, but strange. The script was influenced by different cultures.

"Hmm, It appears to be a jumbled mix of ideograms from Archaic Chinese and ancient Egyptian. It's weird." I looked up at Tom. He had that faraway look again. I waved a hand in front of him and he didn't react. I could suddenly see as if through his eyes, and hear, or rather feel, his thoughts. It was an incredible feeling inside me. I drifted deeper into yesterday's unfolding experience.

He was staring at something through a misty blue veil. Tom squinted to narrow his vision. He made sure he wasn't seeing things. There was an image of a shimmering face in front of him. I can see her clearly now, with glowing golden-brown eyes and striking features. She was whispering a message that I could not make out. Swiftly, her eyes turned to me. It was as if she saw me and I was not a welcome sight. She vanished, and the veil faded out.

Her eyes were the same color as mine.

Tom shook himself out of his dreamlike state. He straightened, shaking his head, clearly disoriented. I heard him think: *Her statue is in my hotel room. It should be exactly where I left it. Have I lost it?*

Everything OK? Was all I heard myself say. I didn't know what had happened to him, how to process what was happening, what statue he was thinking about. And, I did not want to think about how I could sense his thoughts. It was only a fraction of a second, but it was so intense, so detailed, and so unsettling....

I felt Tom quiver as he came to and his fingers combed through his hair to compose himself. "Ignore my crazy antics. I'm just letting lose after a hectic week. I'm only playing around with you."

Not wanting to acknowledge what had happened, I continued where I left off. "Anyway, Tom, that's only a myth in some cultures. In ancient Egypt, amulets were known to have extraordinary powers. Grave robbers would break into a royal tomb to steal the possessions and amulets worn on the mummified corpse, that were meant to protect the deceased in the afterlife and secure their soul's passage. Legend says that those who committed these grave crimes endured horrific tragedies, until the artifact was returned to its rightful owner."

There's no denying Tom was agitated. His erratic actions were out of character. I knew he had massive undertakings that included fitting me into his life. I could see this was beyond his comfort zone. He was clearly on the verge of a panic attack or something. I needed to talk him down, restore some normalcy.

"But it's probably only an old compact welded shut." For our sake, I eased up on my suspicion of the piece. Tom stared blankly into the room, his mind was still focused on the face he had seen moments earlier, and what she had said to him.

"Tom?" I rested my hand on his shoulder.

"Sorry, what were you saying?" He turned around.

"Oh, it's only an old compact or something. Probably some 1960s retro piece. Sorry to say nothing magical here." But I knew otherwise. An authentic amulet could possess supernatural powers if the spirit inside was awoken. I grew up in a household of artifacts. My parents read me ancient folklore and proverbs before I learned to ride a bike. On my way to the sofa, I placed it on the shiny cherry wood mantel above the fireplace.

"A mid-century modern compact? So, no more curse stuff?" Tom's face softened. "The idea of an ages-old curse is ridiculous, right? This is the 21st century, not medieval times." He told me what Margie had said about it: Great rulers wore meaningful medallions or objects during a crisis or event. It meant power and notability. Who could argue with that?

Tom became restless, moving from the table where he had placed the Ouija board to the fireplace, then over to the window to look out at the traffic below. He was still thinking about that mysterious woman in his vision.

My cat, Baster, jumped up onto the sofa. She curled up beside me. Tom gripped the window's frame, his knuckles turned white, reflecting his tension. Tom was losing a battle with his rational mind. He wrestled with his fleeting thoughts: *Why did I ever go into that tunnel? What got into me?*

It was best to leave him alone for a few minutes, and besides, nature was calling. I walked down the hall to the washroom. When I came back out, I caught a glimpse of his reflection in the hall mirror. He was on his phone ordering a pizza, and his voice was calm as if nothing had happened. I decided to just ignore the whole thing. We all have our moments.

I went into the kitchen and uncorked the wine beside the sink. Tom had picked up a Chardonnay on his way over to my place. It also was beside his computer bag. I reached up for the Waterford crystal wineglasses on the top shelf, and tore off a few sheets of paper towel.

By the time the doorbell rang, everything seemed normal again. It was as if a spell had been lifted and he was the endearing and witty Tom I was falling in love with. We had an early dinner by candlelight beside the fireplace on a burgundy Oriental rug. I left some pizza crust in the box. Tom poured us each a bit more wine.

"Ready Irene?" With a wave of gusto, Tom's arm swept the pizza box aside to make room. He picked up the Ouija board. "Let's see what real ghostly is. Maybe this talking board has something to say. It has kept quiet long enough under a stairwell."

"Don't make me nervous!" I took his hands in mine. "How about a jigsaw puzzle or a computer game?"

"It's only a piece of wood. Let's have some fun. Margie would insist on it." Tom was eager to call in the spirit world by the look in his eyes.

I felt like a stranger in my own home.

"Do not fear. This is your destiny!"

Tom acted surprised by his own words.

I lowered myself onto both knees, beside the board. Tom sat on a cushion on the opposite side, beside the fireplace. He appeared chilled as he rubbed his hands together fast. I contemplated the board's circular display of letters and numbers arranged in a double rainbow arc. My fingers touched the initials carved into its side.

Who was PK? I had seen those initials before but couldn't recall where. Maybe an alleyway graffiti tag or carved into a tree. Tom read out the only rule: never forget to say "good-bye" to the spirits to end the game.

～～～

"That's to cut off contact with the other side!" My voice lowered. Baster watched me intently from the hallway. My parents had told me never to touch Ouija boards. Authentic ones used during real séances were rare and could reveal unsettling truths or unexpected events, even release unearthly powers. But you wouldn't find one hidden in a pile of junk under a stairwell.

I dismissed any lingering notions that festered inside me. This was nothing other than a silly game. I mimicked Tom's serious look and body posture for fun. We placed our fingertips on the edges of the heart shape pointer. Our hands jerked about as the pointer speedily circled around the board picking out letters as we repeated them out loud.

It spelled out: I–R–I–S

"That's my name!" I cried out.

Tom whispered in a voice that did not sound like his own: Iris. It is time.

How did Tom know my birth name? It was not something I had shared with anyone since my teenage years. Like the rest of the world, he knew me as Irene. Is this one of those rare boards with true magic?

Why didn't I trust my instincts and refuse to play this so-called game? Tom didn't move, which made the situation even more unsettling for me. I let go of the pointer and pushed the board away. I inched backward to the far wall and Tom rose to his feet. It was not an easy or a comfortable silence, it was dead quiet.

There was a shift in his stance as his head turned to me. Tom burst into action and his blue-eyed stare filled with purpose. He swooped up the amulet from the mantel and bowed onto one knee. "Might you be the goddess Iris? This is for your journey."

Tom's tone deepened. He rose to his feet. The chain was draped gently around my neck. My heart somersaulted in my chest as the amulet touched my heart. He inched closer, declaring, "My Fleur-de-lis you're a charming Iris flower, with three petals of wisdom, hope, and valor. You have graced this world with an undying love. Your window is now rippling in her wake...."

"I've had enough of this game, stop it!" Dismayed, tears rolled onto my chin. I pushed Tom away. He stumbled over the pizza box, and it flew into the air. Baster caught a bit of crust midair as it flew by. Nothing gets past that feline. My ankle twisted in the commotion. I fell backward as Tom awoke from his trance. He sounded a gripping choke from his contracted throat.

The room went chillingly quiet again. Tom had come to and gasped for air. I felt his heart racing against mine as he pulled me in close.

"Are you all right?"

"You scared me!"

"Sorry, I don't know what got into me. Irene, my head feels as if it's about to explode." Soaked in sweat, he rubbed his arms down saying he felt stone cold. He looked up, his face filled with uncertainty, and panic set in for both of us. We both stood in clothes soaked with nervous sweat. It was the most tender yet totally awkward embrace that we've ever experienced together as we sought comfort in each others' arms.

I changed into an oversized nightshirt, and with a heap of blankets and pillows that I carried out from the bedroom. I made ourselves a nest on the rug beside the sofa as Tom stacked his clothes on the sofa's armrest. We held each other close from fear of the unknown.

No rational thought could calm my rising concern. Tom must be embarrassed by his outlandish behavior as he can't change what had happened. To distract from the late afternoon fiasco, I turned on the television. We watched a mindless comedy until we both fell into an exhausted sleep without saying a word at 7:00 PM.

We both forgot to obey the only game rule.

There is a place that is outside time and space where live the ancient gods.

The rules are an eternal mystery there.

Without time, events move endlessly in no-space. These ripples occur everywhere and nowhere. Its presence is bound by the construct of time's arrow, yet confined to a narrow slice of existence in this universe of ours. Mortal humans cannot conceive of it, cannot fathom its mysterious presence and its ways.

In 1308, on Earth, a German monk named Theodoric, studied and understood the basic physics of the rainbow, and this sent a tremor through these eternal overseers living beyond the luminous arc, as their power is fed from human belief and cultural lore.

In the late 1600s', Sir Isaac Newton explained gravity as a universal force, and later, in 1819, French physicist Augustin-Jean Fresnel won a prize for his treatise "Memoir on the Diffraction of Light," in which he ended for ever the mystery of the edges of shadows.

By explaining the universe scientifically these men and others sought to banish demons, and with them, all the invisible deities themselves. These and other scientific advances on Earth tried to erode the belief of their presence, demystifying the barrier between the gods and the human mind, and destabilizing the very foundations of what the ancient-of-ancients called no-space.

When a rare astronomical event occurred on the edge of this solar system, the thin barrier separating no-space from the mortal realm tore. The cataclysm expelled a goddess from the sanctuary above, into what we call normal time and space. She plummeted into an oceanic pole of inaccessibility, where an undercurrent entrapped her somewhere.

The rules are different here.

- CHAPTER 2 -

Toronto, a millennial growing up

I was named after the mythological figure, Iris: the goddess of the rainbow who oversees the sky and the sea. She is a prophetic messenger through the power of vision. Since ancient times, this legendary icon has been depicted in paintings and sculptures in robes of shimmery hues, pouring pitchers of seawater into the clouds to replenish them.

My parents had met in university, were married by the age of twenty and died together in each other's arms just after turning fifty. That made the local news: their fifteen minutes of fame, not for their lives, but for their deaths.

My father was old-stock Canadian of British and Irish ancestry, and my mother of mixed Dutch and Polynesian heritage. I had inherited a rich mixture of family folklore and mythology. They had studied ancient mythology and mysticism throughout the ages, and both eventually became university professors and worldwide authorities in their fields. Their degrees were complementary, my father's in metaphysical literature, and my mother's in mystical iconography.

Their research had led them to have many friends from all lifestyles. They understood that much of what seemed unexplainable and irrational to one person might be perfectly sensible to another. I learned at a young age to never dismiss a system of belief because I couldn't understand it, or figure out how it works yet.

I'd ask my mother to tell me the story of my birth. She had an enchanting voice that could imitate the poetic-accent of the astrologer, with her accentuated pitches and tones that made me giggle each time. It excited me to hear the story again and again.

She would have me cuddle-up beside her, wrapped in my favorite blanket. When my eyes beamed excitedly, she would touch my nose gently, saying, that my very first breath was taken in a delivery room at a downtown Toronto hospital over three decades ago. It was exactly three decades, four years and three months to be exact as I reflected on the comforting recollection. I'd snuggle in close for the story.

When I was born, my mother's best friend's grandmother, Calliope Delos, from the Greek Island of Kos, sat in the hallway, and not even the most hardened nurses had the nerve to tell her to go back to the waiting room. The elderly, frail-looking turbaned woman was wearing a purple velvet dress with multiple strands of colorful beaded necklaces.

Mrs. Delos pulled her double-pointed knitting needles and a ball of soft yarn, out of the tote bag in the basket of her walker. People passing down the hall glanced over to watch her knitting a baby blanket, with superb dexterity. As a gifted astrologer, all she needed to forecast my future was the exact time of my birth.

"Eureka! I got it!" Her voice echoed down the corridor after she heard my first cry. According to my mother, the following day she dropped by to visit us. With a double knock, she peered into the room. It was our nursing and bonding time, but my mother gestured her in.

"You made it! I hear there's a snowstorm coming."

"I wouldn't dream of being late. Mrs. Montgomery, I have news for you." Mrs. Delos waved a thick folder. She unwrapped her scarf and hung it over her coat on the hook. Relaxed in a soft armchair next to the bed, she clasped her hands ready to get started.

"The stars and planets have a way of talking to me." Her eyes gleamed. "It's that instinctive tingle in my stomach, and right here." She tapped on her temple.

"I see, that's interesting."

"I inherited it from my grandmother and the talent skips a generation. I even have a telescope and compass for tough charts like hers. I stayed up into the early hours to figure out your daughter's lifelong forecast. After I calculated her natal chart, her future started to unravel before my eyes. I'd suggest you prepare yourself. This may come as a surprise."

My mother always emphasized what Mrs. Delos said next: "Let's see, the best place to start is usually at the beginning. But, that's well before this lifetime." Then, she shuffled pensively through a folder full of papers. I always wondered what that meant. Did it just mean Mrs. Delos believed in reincarnation, or did it mean something more specific?

She held up a handwritten paper. "According to this chart, a cosmic event occurred the moment your daughter took her first breath. There was a cluster of seven planets in the constellation of Aquarius, and this stellium bundle is a powerful force in astrology. That is very auspicious Mrs. Montgomery, particularly with her January birth time."

My mother said she scrutinized the chart, but was able to make no sense at all of the squiggly lines and scrawled notes, in a mixture of English and Greek. The astrologer went on to tell my mother that I was the embodied persona of the goddess Iris: the legendary symbol of the rainbow. My mother of course knew about this messenger of the gods to mortal beings.

Mrs. Delos said she had made meticulous calculations, and there was no doubt that I was made up of the same Zodiac energy as Iris. This water-carrier sign called Aquarius had a strong influence my first breath. *doubt*

But my future was a little less clear. With her self-assured expression, she said without a double, it was empirically evident that it would be a few decades before my destiny would unfold. It would be triggered by a midlife crisis, though it might not be mine, but rather someone else's crisis, someone close to me.

It would happen with the alignment of Venus, Mars and Jupiter, at the exact moment Earth passes through a stardust trail of a bright blue comet's elliptical orbit. This was a rare event to occur as not only do the planets align so far apart by a fraction of a degree, but this comet is a mystery. It may not be from this solar system.

She said that the resolution of this crisis was a secret the stars would not reveal, but that it would surely be extraordinary. She said small things will occur that I might notice, strange signs around me, the numinous reaching out to me would presage it.

The most important part was that I would not be alone. Whatever this crisis was, I would cross paths with others who would help me achieve my true destiny. Then as my mother told it, the sun poured in through a break in the clouds, melting the frost on the windowpane. There was a rainbow. A winter rainbow. Mrs. Delos declared that it was a sign, a sign that my mother must name me, Iris.

You are my sweet Iris, my mother would say to me, concluding the story of my birth.

I still have the baby blanket that Mrs. Delos had knitted in the waiting room.

I grew up on a boulevard lined with majestic weeping willow and magnolia trees. Our neighborhood was an old money enclave on the edge of downtown Toronto, nestled between a secluded ravine park and Mount

Pleasant Cemetery. A wrought iron fence surrounded our home, built by my mother's great uncle Casper before the first world war, on the site of a pioneer-era inn.

Casper was an eccentric bachelor who made fortunes in oil, boot legging, and racehorses. My mother had always been his favorite, his first and only grandniece, and she inherited the house when she was only three years old.

For his funeral procession, she rode up front with her family in a horse drawn carriage along the downtown streets of Toronto. He was always a spectacle, and even the smallest detail was meticulously planned before his passing. He had specified in his Will that at his funeral his sister—my grandmother—had to wear a replica of Queen Victoria's mourning dress.

There was a painting of him dominating the marble foyer as a severe-looking man in a naval uniform to which he was not entitled, looking out to a storm-wracked sea. It was also a requirement in his Will that his portrait was not to be taken down. The brass plaque on the bottom of the heavy oak frame named him Casper Thomas McGill, and gave the year as 1939. His gaze seemed to penetrate my soul with a sense of anguish I could never understand, so I always avoided eye contact on my way to the kitchen.

Other family pictures and Hudson River School landscapes flowed up the staircase wall and into the upstairs hall. The climate controlled library, to the left of the foyer, had a ladder that slid around an oval room. From mammoth-sized, leather-bound, and foil-stamped books to macro-miniature 16th-century bibles, were all shelved by genre and time period. I would also borrow books from my school library, and I confess that more than a few fines were paid for romances and mysteries that ended up on the shelves at home.

Antiques and statues all had their designated place. There was a vault for rare maps, manuscripts and artifacts. A movable panel concealed a small room that had been built as a bomb shelter during the second world war, but was only ever used to store apples and root vegetables over winter.

There was an escape tunnel behind it, but that door was kept locked and I was never allowed in. My parents told me it was not well-built and unsafe. They had built the gazebo on top of the exit hatch to ensure there would be no accidents. Now, I am not so sure that is really where the tunnel ended.

Off the library there was a sunroom overlooking the landscaped lawn. We'd all read books under the stained-glass windows on Sunday afternoons. The mosaic floor was a sundial excavated from a medieval French castle, brought by ship when the house was built. Nothing was too over-the-top for Casper.

The wine cellar had rows of vintage wines, bourbon, and champagne. Spirits of gin and whiskey from the prohibition days were stored in a locked glass cabinet, never to be touched as requested in her great uncle's

Will. This display was meant to be a memorial to his Michigan rum-running days, in the early part of the 20th century, where he made the lion's share of his fortune.

My bedroom window overlooked the gazebo. It was a beautifully decorated garden structure. I would watch the splendor of summer garden parties, in my velvet party dress. I'd listen to the laughter and music, while feeding peanuts to squirrels on the window's ledge.

My parents had a mural of a starlit nightscape painted on my bedroom ceiling to welcome me into the world. Each of the stars in my constellation, Aquarius, was a light green glow-in-the-dark dot painted with a faint rainbow aura to celebrate my goddess-namesake. Shooting stars and comets enhanced the realism of the vastness of space above me.

Feeling grown-up with proper table manners by six, I accepted my parents' confession that they were unable to have another child. They told me that the stork had many other childless mothers wishing for babies, and we should not be greedy. It was hard growing up alone, without siblings or even neighborhood children my age. I was an only child with few friends from school.

One day, I had an idea. I made a canopy from a sheet draped over my bedpost. In a costume tiara and gown from Halloween, I'd say formal words and adopt my dolls as my siblings. My stuffed animals on top of the dresser drawer, were the guests at all my ceremonies. They all had mythological names, too. I wasn't sure what their names meant, but they felt right. I'd confide in them. They were my friends who knew my secrets. I did this all on my own and in secret, thinking my parents would be upset if they found out.

As a small child, I dreamed of journeying over the rainbow crests with my winged staff of healing powers, just like the goddess Iris. Swift-footed in a flowing gown, my golden wings would carry me over the terrain and the inscrutable seas. But, my wishful belief was shattered. My mother, passing by my room with a load of laundry, saw me trying to soar off the top of my bedpost, plastic wand held high to direct me through my flight.

Looking back, I was fortunate she had caught me midair. My parents sat with me, wiping away my tears for the rest of the evening. I cried myself to sleep on hearing the supposed truth that it was only a myth—a fable, a story, make believe. I was heartbroken by their words, but the little girl part of me never gave up believing the goddess Iris was real. I could feel her spirit within me. Somewhere.

Our house had many rooms and hallways, with a spiral stairwell in the kitchen pantry. I was told it led to the attic, but its locked door forbid my access. When I became scared of my own shadow, during my adventures exploring cedar closets and antique armoires, my parents thought it wise to overcome my fear of the basement.

The light bulb dangling on a wire, over the staircase, served only to accentuate its eeriness compared to the rest of the light-filled house. It cast the most frightful creatures on the walls from the top step. With a few dolls stacked under my arms, I was escorted down the steep descent. Soon, I had them wait at the top of the stairs, while my dolls accompanied me on my adventure.

My parents were both brought up on stories of ancestors, who came by boat from the old country, to escape persecution and famine, and those who went through the world wars and lived to tell the tales. They said that these stories had taught them that fear was only in your mind and needed to be conquered. They were fearless.

I only saw them scared once, the day they died.

To train me to think outside the box, and to expand my intellect, they encouraged me to draw outside the lines especially in my coloring books, under the twinkling stars on my ceiling. I felt at home under the replica of the heavens as I slept.

The constellations of the Zodiac family watched over me even on the cloudiest night. The twelve star-signs imparts guidance with their strategic moves amongst themselves as the stars and the planets shuffle about.

As for me, I'm an Aquarian child, I had a water-pitcher like the rainbow goddess, but I would pour vital healing energy into the clouds. I felt, I too, was a messenger between the invisible deities and people, their worlds separated by a colorful arc. My worldly hues inspire all of Nature's magical creations around me. And, I'll never forget one vivid dream of a captain lost in a storm.

The importance of education was valued in our home as a priority growing up. So, mother planned my bedtime stories out in advance for each year. I learned about classical archetypes and metaphors before I was taught how to ride a bicycle, or began piano lessons.

My coloring books featured the ruins of Pompeii, Egyptian temples, and human evolution. These classic, fabled stories were lavishly illustrated 19th-century editions of Homer's poetic Iliad and Odyssey, myths of ancient Egypt, and Martin Gardner's annotated Alice in Wonderland. As I grew older, a thumbtack held my reading list on a corkboard in the kitchen, and it never had fewer than seven books each week.

The age of ten was pivotal for me. I was introduced to the mystery of the universal binary code of a 1 and a 0 in limitless sequences. Father unleashed the secret of this knowledge, with his usual enthusiasm. They're the only numbers used to create all technology, with its millions of sequences and patterns. And, the same two numbers probably built the structure of the universe and everything in it, too.

I wasn't sure if he was serious about the binary mathematical equations that make up everything in the world. But, by his wink, I had a hunch it was a huge topic for future research. So, I'd study the star sequence patterns on my bedroom ceiling and connected the dots.

I thought I knew everything. Childhood seemed like it would never end. But the end always comes, and with it, your destiny awaits. Your turn will come, father would say. That's fate, there's no denying it, mother would agree.

One year all my school friends had a romance. For me it happened over the summer break. I felt like I was a heroine in a good romantic movie. Under lock and key, my journal entry in my diary was written at overnight camp, where I fell head-over-heels for a cool guy on a canoe trip. It happened in a tent near a cliff after the campfire burnt out. How romantic is that?

Even his sister was great. Sally and I became BFFs, my first. She was only eleven months older than me, and although we lived in different cities, we shared a lot of the same interests.

But summer ended, and I returned home after two months away, heart-broken. But, I looked forward to the Canadian National Exhibition, with its finale: The Labour Day Parade that faithfully announced the close of the summer season. The first parade was held in 1872 in support of the Toronto Typographical Union.

And as for Sally, my BFF, her family lived in Montreal. It was a six-hour drive from Toronto. Despite cell phones and email and all the other means of staying connected, distance still mattered in those days. By the first snowfall, we had forgotten about each other. I never would have imagined in my wildest dreams that our lives would cross paths again.

After I finished high school, I legally changed my name. My parents were supportive as I was of age. And, mother believed it was part of my fated destiny to blaze my own trail however I see fit. I believed that I had control of my future and had dismissed Mrs. Delos's predictions as the ramblings of a superstitious old woman. I marched onward, independent, and with a new identity: Irene Montgomery.

In my early twenties, I was living on a scholarship. I also had a part-time job as a waitress at a family run restaurant. I received my degree in anthropology, but my career path took on a life of its own. It veered into a behind the scenes career in the fashion industry.

My studious ambitions made my parents proud and I stayed very close with them. We would get together every Wednesday night for dinner and a movie at their house. Sometimes I would sleep over in my old room, dreaming under the painted stars, with my forgotten diaries buried in the bottom drawer of the nightstand.

In my mid-twenties, I was dating a charming executive in the airline industry. We were a jet-setting couple for a few years. Our five-star getaways included: Manhattan, Las Vegas, and coastal resorts within a six-hour flight. I was living in a chic industrial–style loft. He was supportive of my ambitious nature.

I was a soundscape developer for a Toronto-based fashion house. I was their top melody attuner. I also led the sound image team for the company's expansion nationwide. Their expectations were high with me on-board, with the potential to license their proprietary technology throughout North America.

The pay was decent, and it more then covered my lifestyle. Big things were promised if the company's drastic revamp strategy of their brand took off. We were all confident it would by the holiday season.

Overall, my position and responsibilities were incredible. They allowed me to utilize my talent, using my excellent ear and sense of the mystical to develop unique, instantly recognizable soundscapes for the company's retail and digital outlets as well as a social media advertising campaign.

The cataclysm in no-space rippled through our universe. In every generation and in each culture, a personified Iris was born to leave behind a folklore of her experience. Many lived normal lives, others achieved greatness, and some lived in quiet desperation. But all left an indelible impression upon humanity in a ripple of time.

Zephyr and Bastet, the gods dispatched to bring goddess Iris back to the no-place, sought to heal the rift and reclaim their lost companion. They searched the Earth with their presence felt more than seen.

The ancient-of-ancients mortals that roamed on Earth called them the "Invisibles." The deities' names were revealed in prophetic dreams. They spoke of them in cryptic scriptures on parchment and hieroglyphs carved into stone.

The Invisibles felt their way from ripple to ripple, gradually homing in on the core of the rift. They would embodied their essence into atmospheric conditions to influence weather patterns for their needs. But, they knew the ripples would need to heal before the main rift could be repaired, and the rainbow goddess brought home again.

~~~~~

- CHAPTER 3 -

Toronto, December 2014

It was early December. The city covered in a light fringe of snow, with the excitement of holiday shopping and celebrations were in the air.

This was an evening, I'd never forget. Elated with my atmospheric melody creation, approved for release today, I took in the city's magical light displays as I headed over to my parents' house for movie night. Billowing clouds of black smoke put me into a state of shock. A series of small explosions rocked the neighborhood. Fire trucks came screaming past me. They turned down the street to the blaze that was consuming my family home.

As I ran up, screaming for my parents, a police officer intercepted me. I turned around to face him. Once he realized I was the owners' daughter, he started to interview me in case I knew anything the firefighters might find useful, such as locations of potentially explosive chemicals stored on the site, and the number of people and animals in the house.

The officer said that it appeared that a car had lost control on a patch of black ice, skidded through the fence and across the lawn, that was covered in an inch or two of snow. Passing through, it had severed the gas line for our barbecue, that my father had moved to the gazebo for garden parties. The driver regained control and drove on, oblivious to the devastation that was about to literally explode in his wake.

I saw my parents through the blackened smoke, though the paramedics later insisted was only my imagination, from stress-induced trauma. They were in their bedroom window, locked in each other's arms, afraid.

Instinct drove me to run into the house to rescue them. I was soon surrounded by flames myself, choking, disoriented. I had become oblivious to the flames, and uncle Casper's portrait—on fire in its heavy oak frame—fell on me, trapping me, shattering my ankle, and dealing a ringing blow to the back of my head.

I was rescued by a heroic firefighter, who stayed with me as the paramedics treated my burns, and assessed my broken bones and concussion.

I still send her a thank-you card every year.

My parents were not so lucky.

The fire trucks, paramedics, and police blocked off the street for what seemed forever. The blaze was extinguished with great effort. An excavator eventually being brought in to level the smoldering timbers to make sure new hotspots would not flare up.

I was in intensive care for two weeks.

All that still stood when I was released from hospital was, ironically, the cinder-draped remains of the gazebo, and the library vault. The scent of smoke and destruction lingered in the air. Everything was dusted with fresh snow, making for surreal post-apocalyptic scenes.

Memories of growing up in this house came to mind as I picked my way on my crutches through the rubble, with the fire department's safety officer, a month later. The kitchen with its stone hearth was now reduced to a heap of blackened granite cobbles. The marble-floored entry hall had nothing left to mark the grand staircase, but a charred newel post. The library and its sacred books full of ancient mysteries was located by the charred but still intact steel vault of rare manuscripts and artifacts.

Everything else vanished overnight.

Stepping around the vault, I found the entrance to the bomb shelter, and the tunnel behind it, cordoned off with flimsy yellow tape that couldn't keep me out.

I poked my head into the opening as a gloved-hand touched my shoulder. The safety officer offered me his flashlight. We entered together. It was musty and damp. The officer seemed intrigued as not every house fire revealed a secret tunnel. Wood planks propped up the walls at intervals, like the 1800s mineshaft timbers in the movies. We were both amazed it hadn't caved in over the past century. Trails of furry moss snaked up the walls of the tunnel, and deep tree roots draped down.

After a short distance inside, the officer acted startled. We had put ourselves in danger. He had no idea what overcame him to take me inside. With his cap tilted down, the officer escorted me out by my elbow as his pant leg snagged on a nail sticking out of one of the support planks. He stumbled forward, releasing my arm. A small cascade of rocks and mud fell around his foot. I saw him trying to pull himself free of the nail as more debris, and an ominous creaking of the timbers, warned of an impending collapse of the tunnel. The ground shifted from under me.

He shouted at me to not look back. Frightened and despite the crutches, I made it out fast. A plank crashed down behind the officer, and the passage started to cave in. He flew out of the tunnel as if blown out by a blast. I never did reach the end of the tunnel under the gazebo. The passageway had seemed much longer than the thirty feet from the house to that structure's charred skeleton, and we had not even reached the end.

When the tunnel collapsed, the asphalt of the street cracked intermittently along a long stretch of roadway, suggesting the tunnel continued well past the bounds of my parents' property. And I once heard a story over a marshmallow cookie sandwich at Khilto's, that its own sealed trapdoor rattled that day, even though it was several miles away.

The officer was in shock, glassy-eyed and speechless. A higher-ranking official ran toward him. "What got into you to go in there? That was incredibly dangerous. You barely made it out alive and risked the lady's life. Safety regulations are there for a reason."

~~~~~

Confused, the officer shook his head, insisting there was an invisible force in the tunnel. He described it as a blue angel that had freed his leg and carried him out to safety. A friend of mine who worked at the local police station later told me that he was released from the force, with an early pension less than a year later. They thought he had lost his mind in the tunnel. But, one thing's for sure, an unknown part of Toronto's history was swallowed up into the earth that day.

The fire department investigators treated the fire as the accident it was and closed the case. The insurance company declared that the damage was uninsurable, because the barbecue's exposed gas line was longer than allowed by code. But they did pay out my parents' outdated, minimal life insurance policies. It was enough to host a memorial service suitable for two beloved professors, but not much more.

I donated the contents of the vault, minus their personal papers, to the Royal Ontario Museum. I don't think any of it ever went on display, but I am sure some academic curator will, one day, spend quality time with those ancient artifacts and maps. I sold the land to a developer and used some of the proceeds to pay off my parents' debts. I locked most of the rest in investments.

Where my family home once stood, an exclusive retirement home complex was built. Where the gazebo once was, is now a manicured lawn bowling and croquet greens. It is surrounded by stately courtyard furniture for seasonal dining and garden parties.

~~~~~

During my recovery period, I remember a cascade of thoughts: inspirations and ideas, day and night. A friend had given me a journal. It was unlined, heavy, slightly yellowish linen paper, bound in blue sailcloth, with the impression of a leaf on the cover. A reminder of my diaries growing up. At my therapist's suggestion, I started to write down my experiences. The nightmares of the fire eased-up. My journal soon became a chronicle of the goddess Iris and a sea captain.

I would fantasize of the goddess pouring a pitcher of seawater into the clouds as a directional wind stirred up the waves to help or hinder the progress of the sailing ships that plied the ocean in the olden days. Then, I'd imagined how she would cast a rainbow after a stormy night for a captain whom she had rescued at sea.

This captain was vivid in my imagination. I first saw him in a dream, when I was a child of six. He appeared as a brave man with a hearty rolling laugh. The captain had blue eyes with windblown hair of charcoal dark and silver wisps. He stood tall before me in dark clothes crusty with salt spray, and his big hands showed the strength of a conqueror. But, his face spoke of a heart that was broken.

While I'd journal, his face would appear before me. I would write down his words that came into my head. The goddess would also appear on occasion in a luminescent pearled robe. It was no longer just a tool to help my recovery, it was becoming notes for a memoir.

When the numbing throb of the concussion eased, a gray cloud still weighed heavily on my shoulders. My longtime boyfriend had dumped me upon hearing the news. A text binged as soon as I left the hospital. I had just turned on my phone for the first time since being hospitalized. He couldn't deal with the situation, and was distraught by his loss. His loss? What....

The message was crystal clear. I had misjudged him for a compassionate person. I was devastated. His deceitful tendencies were camouflaged by his declarations of a selfless, undying love for me. But knowing that didn't help the emotional heartbreak on top of everything else.

Learning to walk again without crutches took several weeks, and adapting to life with a hearing aid took even longer. I realized how fortunate I was to have enough money to be able to afford the very best in physiotherapy, and a hearing aid that's compatible with other devices.

But my life had changed drastically, and the physical recovery felt much quicker than the emotional recovery. Some days I felt like I would never find the old Irene again, or feel relaxed and carefree as I used to. My fears were heightened, and the unknown scared me in ways it never had before. It wasn't just dark alleys, and moving shadows that made my heart leap into my throat. Loud noises, flashes of unsuspecting light at night, and sometimes even strong smells could make my heart race with irrational post-traumatic stress.

My life balanced fragilely on a tightrope. At times, I didn't know which way to turn for help, but inward.

My right ankle would never fully heal, with metal implants holding the fractured pieces of bone together. It would always require extra attention as one wrong move would lead me to stumble at inopportune times. And now nearly deaf in my right ear, from the blow to my head, I would probably need a hearing aid for the rest of my life. But at least my burns were minor, and the only ones with permanent scars were hidden under my clothes, or concealed by my shoulder length hair.

With my hearing loss, I could no longer design soundscapes. The fashion company regretfully let me go, with a gift of shares that might one day be worth something. I needed to reassess my life, maybe make a longterm plan. I no longer had any income, but I did have enough money from the sale of the estate's property to set myself up in a modest downtown condo, and put myself through graduate school.

I decided to follow, not quite in my parents' footsteps, but close. I enrolled in a PhD program in Cultural Anthropology, with one of my mother's friends as my academic advisor. I was prepared to immerse myself in my thesis topic, in honor of my parents' belief that was instilled in me: the reality of the mystical realms. Surely it would distract me from feeling sorry for myself. Soon, my research and scrupulous attention to detail took precedence over unproductive thoughts, and my woe-is-me attitude as my life began to change. And better, I soon had a new-old BFF. It went like this....

I had joined a wellness studio that my physiotherapist had recommended for ongoing activity to maintain balance and flexibility, after the formal treatments were over. I loved it, and the thrice-weekly routine had become my main escape from my intensive research.

It was a warm Tuesday evening. Hungry and sore were the telltale signs of a good class—that was me all over. I had made my usual stop at the grocery store on my way home. In line at the cash, my ankle twisted as I stumbled onto the shopping cart of the woman in line behind me. I whacked my chin on the rim of her cart. She helped me get up from the floor, and offered a bag of frozen berries from her cart. It eased the pain in my jaw. I managed a half-smile from the gesture, grateful for her kindness.

Then we realized we had known each other years before at camp. It was Sally! Older, though not as beat up as me and still pretty fresh looking. The stars must have aligned too as if we were destined to meet each other at that moment in our lives. Sally had moved to Toronto, first for a contract position. But, it wasn't long before she realized how much she enjoyed the excitement of its rich multicultural heritage. The arts and entertainment this city had to offer was what she was looking for.

She was employed at an animation studio. They mostly made short clips for television ads, but the studio also had a couple of major projects including a children's show about a queen bee called Zeetumah, that was rapidly becoming popular on satellite TV networks.

Sally was a creative genius and lead artist for the show, working with the story writers to bring the animated characters to life. She practically lived and breathed the world of bees, and even carried her first hand-drawn sketch of Zeetumah in her wallet.

She had a busy social calendar outside of work, but it felt like we picked up where we had left off. And, we have been BFFs again ever since. I could always count on Sally to be there for me, and I for her.

It was a win-win.

In Austria, in the Middle Ages, a prince was born named Frederick. Sickly as a child, he grew to be a strong emperor, but died young in battle, saving a young girl named Iris from capture by the Mongols.

During the Reformation in England, a boy named Thomas saved a kitten from drowning, and the cat later became a companion to a girl named Iris that saved her from a house fire.

But these were the smallest and most distant of ripples. The main event was reflected on Earth by an oceanic volcanic eruption. A rare diamond-bearing kimberlite shot through the Earth's crust, carrying with it the fallen, frozen form of the goddess. The time was 1820, and the place was off the South Pacific Island known as Oyster Secret.

There were no seismograph or satellite technology to observe the spectacle. Only a sea captain and his crew witnessed it on their way to an island to trade beads and baubles for the precious pearls the natives found in the bay.

Captain Pearl, named for his trade, saw the boiling sea erupting a pillar of smoke and steam, gathering lightning and fierce winds. He knew by his quivering bones that some primeval power had entered the world.

In this world as the storm raged on, the goddess' essence was splintered in three.

Until these three fragments were brought together again, goddess Iris would not be whole. She was nearly helpless in this atmosphere unable to return to no-space.

- CHAPTER 4 -

Toronto, spring 2021

Crammed books spilled out of the bookshelves as paper stacks occupied each corner in every room. I was living my research of obscurity in ancient myth culture. Six years breezed by buried in comfort food wrappers. When I began to see double immersed in fact-checking, it was a sign to take a screen-strain break. Then, the same festering question would pop into my head: am I capable of falling in love again?

The message was coming in loud and clear lately. Actually, it was a thunderous roar between my ears.

But, the remnant feelings of being betrayed and abandoned was still a moot point, with its lingering memories of a life that I once had. It was only a month after being released from hospital, I had heard from a friend that my ex-boyfriend was vacationing in West Palm Beach with a blond, well-heeled corporate banker. She had bumped into them at a beachfront resort, after their couple's massage. It was a familiar romantic interlude that we had indulged in, to escape the last signs of winter in the city. The news sent me spiraling into depression.

To console my tears from my reminiscent longing for what was, a recent habit of mine, I made a vow to ease up on listening to world news for my own sanity, as it only triggered pangs of loneliness, with no end in sight.

Summer was a scorcher, and as usual, my antiquated air conditioner conked out in a heatwave. With a whirlwind of social-distancing and self-quarantine rules, I couldn't find a repair person to come to my home. In an attempt to move forward with cautious optimism, I decided to go over the numbers with my bank's investment advisor. The COVID pandemic had caused more long-term damage to my high-risk portfolio than I had thought.

I was faced with a stark choice: either start dipping into my capital, which was not my first choice, or get a job. It need not be a C-suite position, but I needed a steady, minor source of income to supplement my investments, or else I would have to look for a less expensive place to live, and ease-up on my spending habits.

In theory, the work idea sounded easy enough, but where do I start looking? I had no desire to learn new skills through virtual classes. I had recently completed my thesis on: rainbow deities in ancient scriptures. Now, a part-time job, where I could utilize at least some of my knowledge would be perfect for me.

With periodic public health advisories and lockdowns still hammering the economy, jobs were hard to come by. But I had been to Khilto's many times during the research of my own ideas for the thesis, and knew the aging owner was looking for someone familiar with his customers' esoteric interests to cover the midnight shift.

On my way to Khilto's, one block from the store, there was a construction site, where heavy equipment had started the demolition of a row of old run-down tenement houses. This was in preparation for digging, what would eventually become, a six-story deep pit. Large billboards proclaimed that the site would soon host a new condo tower, soaring to dizzying heights.

We were meant to believe it would somehow be better and more luxurious yet less expensive, than the rest of the downtown condo forest. But, clearly that was just advertising as was the incredibly attractive young couple lounging in the architect's rendition of a marble lobby.

Strutting back and forth, as if guarding the construction site's gate, was an orange and white striped cat. Larger than most cats, she seemed to stare at me with a familiar intensity, inviting me—almost daring me—to cross the street, and introduce myself properly.

As I crossed the street with each step, the skyline became curiously more and more surreal. Structures and textures in my visual periphery took on an altered, somehow almost artificial look. The cat's stare kept me mesmerized, calling me to walk further along the pavement, as she strolled slowly toward an alley at the side of the construction site.

Natural colors blurred into muted grays despite the still bright late afternoon sky. The landscape degraded into line art on what appeared as transparent film before me. Flattened black ink drawings of buildings turned into smoke rings and reappeared elsewhere.

A sudden wave of pressure shot behind my eyes. I felt my face wince recoiling in pain, and it was gone. The sidewalk jolted sideways under me. My heart raced as I wobbled on.

What was happening? Was this an enchantment? A hallucination? Never far from anyone's thoughts these days.... Could it be COVID? It felt so real. Was I fainting? The pavement fluttered under my feet. A rippling sensation moved through me as I stumbled on the crumbling curb.

A slow creaking noise was picked up by my hearing aid. Startled, I looked over at a tall shadow, where the cat had once stood. Then, it vanished quickly between the narrow buildings. I felt the silhouette's stare watch me from an alleyway. I pulled my denim jacket close. Who, or even what, is it?

My mind started making up scenarios. The worried thought that I might never make it home, that this was where I would die, struck me with force. My head was spinning, throwing me off my feet. I managed to hoist myself up onto a concrete traffic barrier that half-blocked the sidewalk in front of the construction site.

The sound in my hearing aid turned into a soft hum, with garbled words that sounded far away. I tried hard to understand them as word in any language represent some form of normality, maybe even sanity.

I knew the message was for my ears only. There was something soothing about it. Something familiar. The monotone acoustics were bewitching, and soon sung me into a calm, detached state. There I sat, waiting, as if for instructions, or for ... something. Waiting.

The ink-line scenery around me splattered into black blotches that changed the landscape. It became a picturesque scene of old Toronto in the early 1800s. I recognized it somehow. It was surreal. Black and white etchings from a clothbound book, lifted away from the pages they were on as the long forgotten memories came to life. People swirled around in the air until they found a place to settle into in the enlivened imagery.

Lightheaded, I gazed through the transparent pavement below me. My consciousness, my very self, sank down through the sidewalk and into the strata of cement, gravel and marine bones in clay. I drifted further down into an tunnel, knee deep in water.

A cooling calm washed over me as I floated above the water watching silent pictures from a hand-cranked antique projector. It cast images upon the rippling surface. The morning rain dampened the spirits of the faces rippling before me. The air smelled pungent as I cringed racked with meddling curiosity. A line of men were struggling to haul crates from a wooden ship, that was lying on its side by the rocky shoreline.

The ship lay near a building, where Khilto's is now. I could see that this is the same building, but it only looked a little different. The windows were smaller and the timbers newer. It doesn't have a plaque over the door. There were several other similar buildings around it. It was just one of a number of warehouses at the old docks.

The cargo the men seemed to be emptying from the ship, looked like crates of dishes and furniture, salt cod, and fine clothing. They were taking it into Khilto's and down into the basement. A place I've never seen before. Two men carrying one particular box wrapped in chains, joked about it being pirate treasure.

One of them signaled they hide it away from the rest deep into the storm sewer that ran past a grate at the back of the storeroom. I knew that they would come back later to open it. As they hauled the chest around the bend under my nose above, I could see through the wooden lid's transparency. I could hardly believe my eyes. It was a statue of a woman with striking features.

Over it all, the voice spoke clearly in my head: *Do not fear as I am within you. You are now a living memory of your future selves.*

The normal early evening streetscape and traffic returned with the last rays of sunset against the skyline, banishing the surreal experience. The words I had heard were confusing and made no sense to me. I wrapped my arms around myself as the streetlights flickered on.

I tried hard to believe this was only a fragmented memory of a late-night movie. Or, my tired imagination was playing tricks on me. But, were the words I heard true? Was this a psychic vision of a snippet of the history of Khilto's a sign that I was destined to work there? Ever since my concussion, I suffered frequent episodes of surrealism in the world around me, that I've come to accept as a normal part of life most of the time.

I carried on across the sidewalk. The tabby cat appeared out of nowhere. I reached out and she started licking the back of my hand, purring. Still a bit disoriented, I had the ridiculous sensation of being a turkey in the oven. But the cat's attention seemed to restore me.

Straightening, I walked gingerly the rest of the way to Khilto's, where the owner was happy to hire me for the 10 PM to 7 AM shift on weekends. When I left the store an hour later the cat was still there, as if waiting for me. She followed me home.

I named her Baster, for the Egyptian cat goddess Bastet, and for that fleeting image of her tongue basting me like a turkey in the oven.

A score of men had set sail with the captain to the South Pacific, to the bay on an island he called Oyster Secret, where the natives dove the clear waters for the largest and best pearls the ladies of Europe had ever seen. They were all experienced sailors, inured to the danger of the seafaring life, but none were prepared for this volcanic eruption.

The captain shouted orders over the howling winds. The mushroom cloud of the eruption was alive with lightning, and unleashed a torrential downpour of salty mud. Crushing waves whipped across the deck, muting the crew's screams of terror. The ship's timbers groaned as it tilted sideways in a sudden whirlpool then capsized, flinging the captain onto the ship's figurehead carved in the likeness of the mariners' goddess that they worshipped at sea.

Pungent salty ozone from lightning strikes prickled his nostrils, and the seawater stung him. As the ship broke apart, the captain clung to the wooden figurehead, and felt it changing in his grasp.

Becoming warm; coming alive.

The captain gasped as the figurehead blinked curiously at his frightened face. She exuded a blue vapor and his brown irises sparkled blue as his dark hair curled. It gave him the energy that he needed to swim, holding onto her. He held her tight, as the waves cast them toward the shores of Oyster Secret.

He was washed onto a sandy patch of the rocky beach, and the statue swept up beside him. She had never felt land, or seen light before from this angle. She watched him crumple over as he heaved up seawater. The captain had survived because she liked him. She would have further use for him.

The carved figurehead settled on the shore, slowly transforming with Iris' presence into some material harder than wood, shrinking to no more than two feet tall. It lay beside the captain's prostrate body.

While a part of the goddess possessed the statue, another part of her was loose, seeking a vessel. That fragment found an ancient Chinese artifact buried in the sand on the beach. The amulet was left on the island of Oyster Secret as an offering for fair winds, by the great navigator Zheng He, on his pre-Columbian voyage of discovery in 1421.

The third, smallest fragment, no more than a spark, floated free of the storm. It was too weak to be bound to any inanimate object, or to have any power over itself, let alone the world around it. This spark found a young woman, halfway around the world, and several generations further along the ripples of space and time.

The few crew that survived found the captain comatose, under the swaying palm trees, and left him for dead. They also found pearls and beautiful conch and abalone shells on the beach. They thought it was the only treasure they were likely to find on this cursed voyage.

If they could persuade the natives to take them in their seafaring outrigger canoes to the nearest larger island, there they could perhaps hail another ship, and the shells and pearls would be enough to purchase passage back to Europe, or to the Americas.

~~~~~

- CHAPTER 5 -

Toronto, autumn 2021

My friend Sally became a weekend regular at Khilto's. She claimed that the ambiance inspired her creative juices to peculate. Adamant, she'd boast, Khilto's own library collection of esoteric eading material contributed to the success of her recent animated series. She was also enamored with a special love interest.

They had crossed paths a few years ago at the waterfront antique market. She watched how Fred bid on a blue and gold Venetian vase at a busy vendor display, and they winked at each other for fun. The vase was a special gift for his sister's birthday.

Sally bumped into Fred rounding a downtown street corner this past spring. He said it was his strong embrace that broke her fall. Sally said he tripped over her exposed leg. They've been together ever since. By autumn, Sally brought Fred by Khilto's so I could meet him.

Fred was a romantic idealist with innocent-looking eyes. Hefty with a square chin, he made a decent living as a stock market analyst for an investment firm, and lived and entertained friends in a trendy uptown loft.

Fred's sister Margie, was five years his senior, and a few inches shorter than him. When Sally first brought Fred around, he had told her about this hidden gem. As a seasoned antiquarian, she had to come see for herself. The atmosphere in Khilto's accented with things-of-the-past impressed her. Margie's sparkling eyes spoke louder than words. She couldn't contain her excitement.

We spoke at length, while Sally and Fred huddled in a corner looking at a book of natural history drawings of insects and plants. Sally's giggling heart-shaped jaw inspired me to open my own heart again. Fred's outbursts of roaring chuckles made us crack up with laughter.

Margie called Fred the yearlong catch, which did not make me feel good for Sally. A woman had twelve months to change her brother's fear of commitment. Even with years of therapy, he still worried tragedy would strike if he planned to marry again, after his fiancée died in a freak accident in his thirties. But, Margie had a hunch that it was different with Sally.

Margie told me all about herself over a cappuccino. After her husband's untimely death, she buried herself in her lifelong passion as an antique collector and dealer. She'd seek out rare pieces, paintings and sculptures, and sell them at antique shows and through exclusive auction houses in Ontario and the Tri-State Area.

A few weeks later, I got a call from Margie. She had heard that an antique store was being sold complete with all its contents, as the owner had passed away, and neither the children nor the grandchildren wanted anything to do with it. The building was a landmark in the city. I knew exactly the place she was talking about as I had walked past it many times, but it was never open.

Margie said her agent explained that the owner was elderly and for the last several years had only opened his door by appointment after his wife passed away. She had called her agent to view the premises, and knowing I had an interest in antiquities, invited me to join her. I would come to realize that this invitation was a pivotal turning point in my life.

Sam, her longtime friend and real estate agent, keyed the door open. "You're going to want to upgrade the security here. This regular door key won't protect all these valuable antiques."

Before the door was wide open, Margie rushed in. With a tug at his coat lapel, Sam followed her. He turned on the light panel as her eyes widened at a portrait in a richly gilded frame. The painting was leaned up against the wall, on top of a gorgeous Georgian buffet.

The rugged handsome captain was posed on the deck of a ship in a storm. He held a woman in his arms. Their unspoken bond mesmerized Margie. She took a step toward the tarnished brass plaque on the bottom of the ornate frame.

"Irene, it's dated 1835. Doesn't say who the subjects are though, just the date. Can you see a signature anywhere? I can't."

My head shook without a word as there was no signature. I examined the waves lashing all around, clouds piling high almost like a tornado, filled with crashing lightning. It made the vessel look incredibly fragile. But the captain and his woman seemed unaffected, serene as if nothing could bother them as long as they had each other. It was a masterpiece. The artist must have been a genius to paint with such depth and emotion.

The captain's penetrating gaze entranced me. He looked like the captain of my dreams in my journal. Could I have seen this portrait before? Maybe my parents had dragged me into this very antique store when I was little. I had seen this haunting painting and it had surfaced vividly again after my accident? This was the only rational explanation I could muster up.

A déjà vu feeling came over me. I looked closer at the woman as Margie's voice plummeted me back into the moment. "Irene, that's odd, isn't it?" Her finger floated over the seaman's head at a small spot that looked transparent. A missed paint stroke? Impossible, but my finger couldn't resist the temptation....

The front door blew open. It rattled hard as a draft swept into the room. Distracted, I swung around and watched as Sam latched the door shut again, tut-tutting some more about the flimsy and inadequate security. The draft combined with the picture's torrential downpour gave me a sympathetic chill. I backed away slowly from the portrait with my hands tucked into my back pockets.

Sam began to inspect the premises with the trained eye of a real estate agent, in search of problems. The store had a central room that led into three smaller display areas. A window high up on the wall rattled in the wind. A long rod hung down for opening and closing it.

"No wonder it's still so chilly in here!" Sam was eying the source. "I can handle this easily enough." He stood up on his toes and forced the window rod up to close it, cutting off the damp breeze. He signaled us to follow him into the office at the far end of the room. And to Margie's surprise, inside there was a small door that was left ajar by a bronze doorstop.

The door opened with a slight push.

A beam of light shone through a tiny roof window that revealed narrow wooden stairs that led up to the attic. She took the lead excited about the make–shift skylight. With each step, we stirred up the dust in the light. The floor planks groaned underfoot ladened with vintage clothing, antique toys, and decorative items.

Back down in the main room, the center aisle was narrow with antiques crammed in on either side. We squeezed our way around the furniture covered in lampshades and ornaments. There were open and sealed boxes. Porcelain tableware was stacked high on a table. Margie's finger cleared a long path through the dust atop a mahogany buffet. A telltale sign it had been closed for years until the estate was finalized. There was plenty of work to be done to bring this place back into its glory again.

"Oh Irene, Sam, follow me, that door must go to the basement. I bet there are hidden secrets down there too. It's a treasure hunt!" Margie quickened her pace to the alcove, where she had to squeeze past a desk to reach the door. Sam used his hips to heave the barrier aside and stepped in. I was right behind him.

Margie fiddled with the crystal doorknob until the door squeaked open on its rusted hinges. She held onto the rail along the cement wall as her eyes tracked the steep uneven stairs to the bottom step. The rush of musty air piqued her curiosity. "I can sniff out hidden relics and spirits too. Irene, my intuition never fails me."

The pull chain on the light socket rattled as Sam yanked it. The bulb cast light onto the cobwebbed wall. He lifted his collar up around his neck. Spider webs and its occupants made him skittish. He wasn't taking any chances of overreacting, especially in front of Margie. Sam cleared his throat. "Ladies first."

"I came equipped for the inspection." Margie pulled a flashlight out of her shoulder bag. Her figure bent low with each step as she dueled excitedly with fallen cobwebs. The flashlight swayed to and fro at the bottom of the staircase. She spotlighted scattered pallet planks that had evidently been used to raise things off the damp floor. There was a rusted drain in the middle of the room. The floor was not all concrete, some parts were cracked tiles, others dirt and clay.

The low ceiling had massive cedar log beams with shreds of bark still hanging down, and the walls, where they could be seen, were mixes of stone, brick, and concrete. Sam's shuffling shoes sent swarms of spiders into dark crevices under wood crates, broken chairs, and rusted chandelier chains.

"This place needs an exterminator!" Sam was clearly skittish with his darting eyes. "There may be bigger pests lurking around so watch your step ladies." He started inspecting the ceiling, tracing wires and pipes, making mental notes.

"The electrical service probably needs upgrading. Looks like you have some old knob-and-tube wiring, not too surprising in a place as old as this. That will need to be looked at. You can't run a modern security system off old wiring. The insurance company will insist on upgrading it right away." Sam shielded his face from the flashlight as Margie came over to inspect it.

"Oh, Sorry Sam! I do appreciate your help. Be a dear, won't you? Can you check with the land registry office for any drawings, maps, or other records? I would love to know more about the history of this building and neighborhood."

"Consider it done Margie."

"I suspect there's a root cellar back behind there. Maybe a crawl space too." Margie gestured at a board wall behind the furnace. "It was common during the last century. Once this place is cleaned up, I'll take a closer look around. Let's make sure there are no old liens on the property."

～～～～～～

Back upstairs she struck a proprietary pose against a wood post. Sam and I both knew it was a done deal. She looked up at the rustic ceiling beam. "The crystal chandeliers in the basement can easily be repaired. They'll look marvelous hung over the central aisle. But there's so much repair work needed. Sam, please have that reflected in the offer price."

"This is what you asked for, Margie. The store has goodwill too. It's a family business passed down for generations. The children and grandchildren that inherited it have no interest in running an antique store, but the Will specifies that's what it must be. They can sell, but only if the place remains in business as an antique store, and it has to keep the same name: Gora's House of Antiques. Now's your chance Margie, it'll change your life."

Those words sealed the deal.

In a few days, the papers shuffled in her fingertips. Margie pulled out a fountain pen she had inherited from her father that she used for all–important documents.

The offer was signed and the deal closed.

Margie spent several weeks sorting and cataloging the store's contents, cleaning out junk, identifying repairable damage to furniture, and contracting the repairs and restoration that were needed. A building inspector dropped by to approve the renovation plans, which included an all-new upgraded electrical service, modern plumbing and thanks to Sam, top-notch security. Margie wanted goods to leave the store through sales, not theft.

Margie had movers take all the larger furniture away to a storage locker. A convoy of pick-up trucks pulled up in early January with the contractor and his crew. They started in the basement and worked their way up. She had spent the money to have it done right. While the work crew transformed the store, she had taken home a carload of small items to clean and polish: crystal, silver, and ornaments.

When the renovations were finished, Margie had the steamed-cleaned, upholstered furniture moved back into the premise. She dusted and polished up the fine wood pieces. The small items were sorted into collections and placed into the showcases. Items were spaced out around the rooms and organized by period and theme. For the grand opening gala, the front room displayed Canadiana furniture for its ambiance of the old Toronto she had grown up in. A circa 1800s general store counter of polished chestnut served as the sales desk.

"If my late husband Abner, could see me now." Margie was elated with her accomplishment. "It's almost complete just one last touch." She watched as Sam climbed up a rickety stepstool on the front porch. He screwed on the newly repainted sign: Gora's House of Antiques as the neighboring storeowners watched on. Tulips and crocuses were almost ready to break through the last vestiges of snow in the front yard flowerbed.

Early March had finally arrived. The neighborhood business association welcomed her with terracotta planters for her porch placed beside the bench and rocker on either side of the screen door. They knew a good business would be good for their businesses too.

Margie's inventory would appeal to the budget conscious treasure hunter and locale clientele to other antique dealers and commission-based interior decorators. Her window display would change weekly. A crystal bowl of shiny trinkets priced under ten dollars sat on a pedestal beside the umbrella stand. People were enticed to step into her store and browse around.

Margie had planned to open her doors without a website, or any other Internet presence. She wanted curiosity seekers to come into the ambiance of her store and touch nostalgic works of art from the past. However, local newspapers and radio stations were sent a hand-delivered press release about the opening only hours before the doors opened to welcome the waiting guests.

This rejection of the web ironically caused a social media frenzy among antique collectors: No virtual presence? Only a brick-and-mortar store? It's a social media hoax! News circulates fast in cyberspace. Buyers were pressured by their discrete clients to attend the grand opening with an authorized, open checkbook policy. Gora's House of Antiques became an overnight success, with her ingenuity and tact.

Margie had a keen business sense and an eye for rare collectibles. She wanted her clients to be discriminating people, on the hunt for unique and original treasures from around the world. But, even more shocking was that the store would be closed during her buying trips.

City officials were excited that she was continuing to operate under the Gora's name, and agreed to designate the building as a heritage site. With their blessing, she commissioned a brass plaque commemorating a structure originally built as a general store built in the 1800s, then occupied briefly by a funerary store until it became Gora's House of Antiques in 1918. It had stayed under that name for over a hundred years.

The captain was found by the islanders who carried him to their village. He awoke weather beaten and confused. They nursed him back to health. Soon he was as healthy as could be expected after his ordeal.

The captain kept me with him wherever he went. We were marooned three years on Oyster Secret, and time enough for the captain to fall in love with a native girl by the name of Alene, which in English means dawn sunray. He called her his ray of sunshine and the pearl of his heart.

She went out one day to fetch firewood from the forest and never returned. The captain hunted for her, searching the island and inquiring of everyone he met.

He learned that she had been taken by blackbirders—despicable pirates who tricked or kidnapped islanders into slavery in Australia. There, she would likely be worked to death on a sugar cane or coffee plantation, or forced into service as some slave—owner's mistress.

The captain was desolate, but try as he might, he could not convince any islander to take him to Australia in their canoes. They said it was too far, too dangerous, and they did not wish to become slaves too.

Months later another ship, this one from Spain, came to refill their freshwater supplies at the island, and carried us to Peru.

- CHAPTER 6 -

Toronto, autumn 2021

Tom Adler was more than restless and his newfound habit of stress-eating didn't help matters. But, he couldn't resist the temptation of room service. It evoked a certain comfort: memories of family holidays, and the fun, and challenging times together. He stared at all the half–eaten dishes, stacked up on the cabinet under a wall-mount flat screen. Every other night, he would make a fine dining reservation at the hotel's restaurant. It was his excuse to put on a dress shirt and tie, only to reminisce with his sorrows in a change of scenery.

Tom was anxious waiting for the call.

Autumn's vibrancy was fading fast with the display of dead foliage along the street below. Today's early morning frost on the window announced summer's end. The winter season was moving in. And, with it, there would be even lonelier nights under dreary gray skies in a slush-covered city. Tom found himself in an upscale hotel worried and alone. And, he wasn't ready to meet anyone yet after his failed marriage.

Overcome with frustrating thoughts, his eyes tracked the skyline in the window that overlooked the bustling city from the twentieth floor. The uncertainty overwhelmed him as his palms slammed down against the edges of his laptop. It's only a device as a means of creating and communication. Why break it? It would only be another expense on top of alimony.

Tom looked around the sparsely furnished room. He had never fully unpacked his suitcases in the one-bedroom suite that was leased by the month. Why bother reflecting on what was? It's history now. A stinging sensation from the biopsy distracted him. It reminded him to work toward his priorities, once he'd figured them out. Although the paperwork had been finalized weeks ago, the reality of his divorce hit him hard.

Mid-forties, he was unprepared for this consequence of divorce, and since his aunt had died two years ago, and his kids moved to Vancouver and Ecuador to start their own families, he really didn't have anyone else in Toronto aside from his longtime friends—Fred, and his sister, Margie.

The half-century mark was fast-approaching. Tom reassured himself that he had at least a few good years left, and then became depressed that he would spend it alone. And there's always those what-ifs, that haunted him. He had overcome many challenges in work and with his family. It was only after his marriage crumbled that his world shattered into pieces.

Although they had parted reasonably amicably, his wife left him for a woman. That was hard to come to terms with, especially now that he needed her support.

It was a long time coming. She had waited until the children were grown up, but it didn't make it any easier.

Tom was virile but wondered if his body exhibited any weakness or vulnerabilities. That's why he had booked a physical exam in the first place. Although, he did not have any real suspicion of any problems. There was a knock on the door, and before they could announce themselves, he shouted to the cleaning staff that every other day is fine.

After they left, Tom swung the door open to place the door hanger sign on the outside handle. He wanted to be left alone and pace around the room two or three times then sit down, wait ten minutes and repeat. He knew it was not uncommon for a man his age to have a prostate scare, based on statistics. But nothing that he heard or read eased the worry.

The specialist would sent the results by noon.

The news? My life is over, maybe—or maybe only a phase of it. Nerves on edge, heat rose in his chest below his weekend stubble. Tom loosened his shirt, and eyed the candy tin on the table beside his early morning coffee, with a layer of lumpy powdered creamer. He slit open the tin's wrapper with his thumb, and tossed the cellophane aside. Despite being warned about sugar, and his higher-than-normal blood pressure, sweets pacified his stress.

In front of the blaring screen, Tom flipped through the channels absentmindedly. He shifted about on the hard couch seat. With a leg swung over the armrest, he nestled into a spot. Glassy-eyed, he turned to face the window barely registering the faint outline of the sun glowing in the feathery clouds as a sports broadcaster waxed enthusiastically about something.

In the corner of the window ledge a spider froze. It had caught his stare and a question came to mind, about what went on behind the beady eyes of an insect. *There is more to life than glass and concrete and gloomy skies,* he thought, *and surely the spider's problems were as important to the spider as his own problems were to him.* He had only blinked and the spider was gone. It had calculated its exit strategy and moved on. Tom nodded blankly in recognition of the good advice. Move on.

Tom's body flexed into full alert, his eyes went wide with fear of whether to check the phone that binged in his shirt pocket. Was it a doomed text message? He paused … then his fingerprint unlocked the phone. Relief washed over him from the single line of text. The news from his specialist gave him a new lease on life, and with it, enthusiasm for living.

With a high-five in the air, he slid down onto the carpet, his knee slammed into the glass table. In happy tears, he comforted it as the phone rang on the table. He looked at the digital display on screen. It was Fred calling. Who else? He answered on the second ring.

"Hello, feeling great, thanks for asking."

"OK, I can ask but you sound good." Fred was prepared for a timely segue in the conversation.

"Better than ever. My doctor says I'm clear. Can you believe it? Cancer free, it's just a cyst."

"Great news, I was concerned. So my friend ready to start living again?"

"Yeah, what's up?"

"Remember the brown-eyed sweetheart I'm dating?"

"Sally? Of course, it's been a while. What happened?" He knew Fred's roundabout way of coming to a point.

"Glad you asked."

"Go on."

"I've discovered a treasure nestled in the heart of our city. That's how Sally describes it. She's the eclectic type. Have you checked out Khilto's Metaphysical Bookstore & Café? It's south of Front Street. It's only a few blocks from your hotel. Better hangout than on your couch and hotel lobby. Sally talked me into a cappuccino last weekend, after the theater. I have to admit it was good, even though I am more of a double–shot espresso guy. It came with a wickedly delicious muffin. It's the owner's secret recipe."

"Sounds good."

"Anyway, there was a fortune-teller in the store. She wore the part. You know, draped in scarfs and beads, and her fingers were loaded with rhinestone rings. We walked up to her and she spoke in this bouncy rhythm accent: 'I'm an authentic gypsy psychic reader.'"

"OK, interest peaked."

"And I'm Fred, was my reply. Sally coaxed me to sit down at her table, complete with a crystal ball and tarot cards fanned-out on a white lace doily. Can you believe it? I can spot a charlatan anywhere. I sipped my fancy coffee, slapped down a twenty, and away she goes shuffle-shuffle with the tarot cards. I cut the deck. She gave me the curled finger cue to push it toward her."

Tom turned on the speaker mode. He placed his phone on the armrest. "Go on Fred, I'm all ears. What does your future hold? You'll be king of the castle?" Fred actually liked the idea. He paused then carried on.

"Cards flew all over the place. She put them in a cross pattern, with a few scattered about the array. Then, she read me. It was freaky, Tom. She started by telling me about my ancestors. People I have only vaguely heard of from my father when I was young. Somewhere out in the Maritimes. I can't understand how she knew so much. Then she told me my future from the cards. The picture images looked scary with words like—Death and Devil—written on them. I almost called it quits with the cards—Hangman and Tower—I can see this fortune-teller being spooky-spooky if she wants too."

"Spooky you say?" Tom clicked the TV off with the remote. "Well, what did she predict?"

"The impossible—but that's why I paid her I suppose. She slowly turned over the last card. With frightful eyes, her hands slammed down. I jumped a little as her fingers strummed the prediction. Her voice lowered as she warned me to stay clear of ocean cliffs. I've never even hiked in the foothills, so that should be easy enough. Down goes her hands again with her wildly crazed eyes. My nerves can only take so much. That's what the cards or the starry heavens or whatever had to say. Oh, and that Sally was my long lost love."

"Really?"

"Get a grip, it surprised me too. Sally was sitting right beside me—her scarf hid her laughing smile. You must be shocked but I have a feeling it's true. Maybe the cards did reveal my future. My mother would say, you'll know when you meet her. God rest her soul, she was a great woman. I feel I'm about to take the plunge."

"I get it, hotels can be a lonely place."

"That's exactly why I called you. Sally has a friend—Irene Montgomery, maybe she's lonely too." Fred paused to play out his move.

There was silence on the other end.

"Yes, Tom, she's shorter than you with shoes on. She has a doctorate in anthropology and works the midnight shift at Khilto's. Imagine that, she has the smarts too. I'm sure you'll find lots to talk about. Politics? Climate change? Alien invasion? Equality in the workplace? You know a little distraction would be good for you outside of work and hotel gift shops."

"You're right, I've been in a slump for too long."

"It's a date. Let's say a match made in heaven as Sally would say." Tom's phone beeped with Irene's cell number and Khilto's address.

It was soon after I adopted Baster that Tom Adler came into my life. But, there was a hesitancy to meet him after our first phone conversation. I had not been out on a date since the accident and the mere thought of being rejected would devastate me. I still had unpredictable muscle spasms in my leg, that could make me seem— OK, not just seem—like an accident-prone ninny.

Fear somehow had a hold over me. Or, it was more of the uncertainty of how he might react to such a public display, or at the sight of my scars. It's been years since I was close to a man or considered a relationship, or even a casual hook-up. I yearned for the impossible: my previous jet–setting world with romance and passion.

What I didn't know was that my predestined fate had begun to unfold since Sally came back into my life. Strange occurrences had become increasingly persistent. Unexpected. Thanks to my father for my proficient skills in binary code, I had begun to see a pattern forming, like the stars in the sky. But what it was? I hadn't figured it out yet. But I will. I always do even if it's too late.

Although many of Khilto's patrons would flirt with me, it was always harmless that I did not take seriously. They would probably have panicked and never returned, if I had shown any actual interest. But Tom was different. He came with Sally's thumbs-up approval and besides, I heard he was incredibly sexy, too.

Why not give him a chance. I had nothing to lose.

Our first date was lunch—authentic Greek cuisine on the Danforth. It was wonderful. We had so much to talk about. By then I was working weekend midnight shifts at Khilto's, and part-time at a florist a few days a week. It didn't take long before Tom awoke what had been dormant in me. I almost forgot those butterfly sensations of being smitten with infatuation, maybe love? We were definitely opposites. It made our encounters exciting and unpredictable. We got together a few times a week.

What he called home during his midlife crisis was a ritzy hotel suite not far from me. He had recently finalized a messy divorce. He had founded his business with his wife, and disentangling their business affairs had left him nearly bankrupt.

By the third date, I knew his life story. Tom was born on a hardscrabble farm near New Liskeard, in northern Ontario. His father was a log-roller for a local paper mill. His mother left them a day after his fourth birthday. He never knew why, but he was sent to live with his only aunt in Toronto. With a name badge pinned onto his summer windbreaker, he experienced his first train ride at the age of four—alone with only one suitcase.

Tom swore it was the school of hard knocks that turned him into a self-made man, and not only his college degree in commerce. Throughout his formal education, he worked part-time to support himself and his aunt. She had to take early retirement due to an onset of a debilitating illness.

Not long after we met, I pressed him to do something out of his comfort zone. Why not bring him into my world of core–strength training? What a disaster that attempt was! It resulted in a restless night for both of us. I had asked Tom to join me for a postural alignment class which, I admit, was my first mistake. I should have known better from Sally's experience. But had I tried to change him? I confess, maybe a little? It's a typical Aquarian thing to do so. I tried to pacify my guilt.

I remember clearly that he had carried both mats and water bottles. We arrived at the studio early. It's only a fifteen minute walk from my place. We entered the studio in silence. Tom followed my lead in spacing out our mats as he looked at an advanced student in the corner contorting and bending into some fairly demanding stretch poses.

The instructor turned on soft music and we began mirroring her routine, at our own fitness level. Tom looked awkward knowing he didn't fit in. He had tried to calm his racing doomsday thoughts. I recalled his face tighten in pain beside me. It resulted in a side cramp as he buckled over from the pose and onto my mat.

Tom looked over the crowd with a last attempt to raise his torso into a side-plank for a leg lift. In his panic a crucial muscle froze as his hips left the ground. Sweating profusely, he somehow propped himself up onto his forearm and got stuck midair. He couldn't move. The spasms were so bad, the group was worried that they might have to call the paramedics.

It took three of us to get him out of the pose. My friends stacked their mats up for him to lie on as his knees bent over an exercise ball to ease the tension in his lower back. He stayed there, unmoving, until the session ended a few minutes later.

With our personal belongings clutched under both my arms, I hustled him away and into a waiting taxi, even though it was only a few blocks to my place.

I wasn't taking any more chances, at least not tonight.

The stairs were a struggle for him. Tom had to climb the last few steps on all fours. He opted for the elevator but it wasn't working again. When he reached the top landing, his hands pressed into the small of his back. I jiggled the lock open with his arm over my shoulder.

Tom's brown coach jacket—along with the mats and water bottles—landed on the floor. I lifted my hair off my neck to cool down. Baster sat in the hallway watching this curious spectacle as if it were a side-show for her amusement. The ceiling fixture flashed then sparked startling me as my finger left the switch.

Darn, the fuse blew again! That's three times this month. The room was still lit dimly by a shaded floor lamp left on. The window sheers drifted as Tom hobbled past toward the washroom down the hall. I draped his jacket over the back of a kitchen chair, and resisted the temptation to rifle through the pockets to see what was clinking.

I lit a row of tapered candles in a crystal holder. It was on the coffee table in the living room. Tom walked over and sank to the carpet beside it. He gingerly stretched out his back voicing grumbles with each breath.

A shaft of moonlight flooded into the room. The dust particles floated in the beam as I fiddled with the knob to ignite the gas fireplace. The embers soon glowed. Slightly propped up on a towel roll that I had slipped under his head, Tom had begun to mold the wax that dripped down the candlesticks, into a shapely sculpture.

I had walked out of the bedroom, with a blanket and a pillow for myself. Tom gave a hard whistle-blow that quenched out the soft-golden flames. The odor of smoldering wax lingered in the air as he loosened his clothes in a vertical position. Tom drifted into a fitful night's sleep of unrest for both of us. I kept an arm's length distance between us for obvious reasons.

The brilliance of the morning sunrise was breath-taking. I watched it from a half-opened eyelid. The sun rose higher, only to splash a golden orange onto the varnished floor beside us, through the sheers. The sunbeam on the windowsill was his morning trigger as his hand spun around to shield his tired eyes from the intense brightness. Tom must have waited for this moment. He pretended to wake with an abrupt snort.

I saw his discomfort with his attempts to get up. I felt his body prepare to try again and this time with oomph. I knew a garbage truck outside had startled him awake an hour earlier, and somehow felt his eyes gazing at the ceiling. A suburbanite for the last few decades, he still wasn't used to downtown living. There's a lot that goes on behind the scenes before the heart of the city wakes up.

With a breathy heave, he managed to pull up the window's wooden frame. I kept still under the blankets, and put on my hearing aid. I heard Tom rummage through the kitchen cupboard. He must be looking for muscle relaxants. The sound of a shaking pill bottle, running water, and a glass clinking down hard onto the counter, confirmed my suspicion.

The aroma that followed a few minutes later aroused my hunger instincts with a stomach gurgle. Despite his pain, Tom was making breakfast. I was hungry and the combined smells of coffee and sizzling sweet butter in a frying pan, brought me to full consciousness.

Irene, are you awake?

I was sprawled out warmly beside the fireplace. My eyes must have revealed telltale signs that I've been awake for hours to protect myself. Tom had tossed and turned all night, and nearly whacked me a few times in his sleep. We had camped out in the living room. That used to be romantic in the past, but last night was for crisis control. Tom's back was wracked in pain. He needed a hard surface to lie on.

There was an uneasiness stirring inside me as I watched Tom place a breakfast platter down in the breakfast nook. It was my favorite sugar high. French toast with maple syrup that we had picked up at a local artisans' market. He was doing his best to please me. Why did I mess up? His face winced with discomfort as his solemn eyes lifted up. I stepped toward him in an untied bathrobe. I was overcome with the feeling of being rejected. It swelled up in me. I didn't have enough distance from my past emotional traumas. Certain words could easily trigger me. My last breakup had devastated me and it was hard to let go of what was.

I moved in close trying to put it out of my mind. My fingers pressed deep into his shoulder muscles then I lightly tickled his back with kisses. Tom turned around to hold me as his hands slipped around my waist. My passionate moves were aroused by his touch.

Our eyes met with mutual desire. With his body pressed close against mine, our hearts beat in rhythm. I rested my head on his chest as my fingertips stroked his upper back. Slowly, he bent over to kiss my head, my brow, my cheeks, my nose, my mouth....

Even after a restless night, his warm breath and seductive kisses set my desire alight for the impossible this morning. I felt his painful twitches with each move. My body rose up onto the toes of one foot, so I could whisper in his ear how sorry I was. He gave a shiver as I spoke my words in a gentle tone. This was his opportunity to say what was on his mind.

By now, I knew when Tom's face was calculating a strategy. He appeared to have analyzed last night's fiasco, by the sparkle in his eye. I knew he felt ridiculous trying to sit cross-legged on a floor, or to bend into an unnatural position for him. He suggested that we explore the city on foot or with bikes. And, why not join him at his fitness club. It has lots of exercise classes and workout equipment. He'll arrange for a personal trainer to get me started. Tom was excited to voice the proposition.

It sounded wonderful! Why not change-up my routine? It's springtime and time to do things differently. Tom powered up his laptop and went online. He upgraded his plan to a couple's membership.

Tom made it easy. He won my heart.

The pills must have kicked in. I heard Tom humming cheerfully in the bedroom afterward. He strolled out dressed in casual work attire and kissed me good-bye. Although it was only 7:30 AM, I knew he had to prepare for an important meeting.

After he left, I leaned my back up against the door. I shouldn't have listened to Sally. A while ago, she had persuaded Fred to join her for a stretch class. It had not turned into the same degree of disaster as my attempt with Tom, but he certainly did not repeat the experience either.

There was something strange in the still silence that made me think about my research on mythological figures and demigods in ancient scriptures. Stories that had left an impression on me. Is destiny only a myth reenacted in consciousness? Baster? Tom? Khilto's? It's more than serendipity, isn't it?

It had clouded over while we ate breakfast as threats of rain loomed. But, I wouldn't let the deteriorating weather dampened my mood. A familiar pungent whiff of a passing garbage truck made me cringe. It was a struggle to pull down the window frame. I returned the bedding to the bedroom and gave a quick tidy up. After Baster's breakfast bowls were replenished and placed on the kitchen floor, I went to turn on the shower.

The hot water had steamed up the room. After fifteen minutes the faucet squeaked shut as I stepped out onto the cold tiles. My toes instantly cramped and my leg stiffened. I grabbed my ankle feeling the bones contort. Snuggled into my mauve fleece bathrobe, my faithful hairdryer did the trick every time.

My foot relaxed into position as my ankle's hardware welcomed the warmth. Then, I applied soothing oil onto the raised surgical scars on my ankle. My robe dropped to the floor. I slathered on body moisturizer from head to toe, then slipped into my flip-flops. With my hair secured in an oversized towel, my nose inched closer to the mirror as I wiped down the foggy condensation. I was in desperate need of a serious closeup look, or should I say inspection of the real me. I tapped on my reflection then it dawned on me. I thought about the timing ... and my starry prediction.

What was my mysterious fate? I conjured up a childhood game: mapping out star coordinates of the constellations, by visualizing the universe around me.

I started to examine the celestial pattern changes that occurred during the Halle-Bopp comet in the northern hemisphere, spring 1997. I was deep in thought as my fingers touched my high cheekbones. I dabbed face-cream on an almost clear complexion. My monthly ritual pimple appeared on schedule.

New star formations have begun to appear since this comet based on my calculations. These coordinates could change our future although it can't be proven. A figurine in the coffee table distracted me. Its reflection caught my eye in the hall mirror. A posed lioness sculpted in wax. It was Tom's creation from last night: a replica of the Egyptian cat goddess, Bastet. Baster brushed up against my legs as it dawned on me. Tom hasn't studied mythological deities. How did he know about Bastet?

But, I was inspired by Tom's creative effort. Months had passed, since I had last made an entry in my healing journal. Tom was a great diversion though. I walked into my bedroom and pulled open the bottom drawer. It was under my keepsake skinny jeans that no longer fit me. My hand smoothed over the cloth-bound journal, I gave the cover a kiss and ensure the captain that I'll add a journal entry after work.

Dressed and ready to face the day, a green light in the corner caught my eye. My phone charger indicated a full battery as I lifted the phone up. I sent a message to the property manager about the recent power outages. The thought of this building turning into an inferno terrified me and with good reason. There must be a short circuit somewhere. Although renovated into condos years ago, it was still an old structure and probably a fire hazard. I listened for the familiar sliding zip sound confirming the message had been sent.

The phone rattled startled me. The property manager responding that quickly? That would be a first. Of course not, it was Sally. She had won opera tickets at a fund-raiser, for tomorrow night. It was just what I needed and we could catch up afterward at a local café. Seven o'clock sharp, outside the Opera House on Queen Street. I loved the arts & entertainment in this city. Sounds like a plan was my reply. With those words, the phone slipped from my ear as I fumbled to end the call.

Darn, not again rolled out as a hiss. My shoulder spasmed and flung the device up to the ceiling. It was all too funny to watch. It barely missed the soapy water in the sink with breakfast dishes. But, it crashed face-down onto the ceramic floor. Alarmed, Baster walked in to inspect the commotion. She spotted the culprit, crouched into position, and pounced on it. With one swipe of her paw, the device shot under the oven.

Baster, you scored again, burst from my lips. My finger shook at her, and she dismissively walked out of the room. She struck a regal pose by the door, upright and on guard. I lowered onto my knees, and with an umbrella swept the phone out from its hiding place.

It was coated in grime and dust balls and shriveled I-don't-want-to-know-what bits of old food from the never-cleaned space under the oven. But the damage

~~~~

appeared minimal, just a hairline fracture to the case. I touched the cracked frame and turned the device on.

With my designer jeans belted fashionably, I was almost ready for my day shift at Theresa's flower shop. My drawer was stuffed with assorted patterned scarves, and a demure shawl from a secret rendezvous romance on a bridge in Paris. That was from my previous life as a soundscape developer for the style-definer and trendsetter, with a jerk of an ex-boyfriend.

This non-reactive thought brought a victory smile to my face. It made me feel alive inside, full of ambition and desire. I took a deep breath, knowing how lucky I was that Tom and I crossed paths thanks to Sally. I looped a silk neck-wrap into shape in front of the hall mirror, to conceal a burn scar on the side of my neck. It had become inflamed with last night's tension, and maybe further irritated by the excitement of chase-the-phone. I reminisced with the sensation of Tom's touch. He knew the right spots to ease my anxiety.

I loved Tom's idea over breakfast of going into the world of innovation and development of a product too. Workouts at his club and spring bicycle rides will be a good test of my stamina and strength. That's if my ankle holds out! Tom's right, take more chances, and there's always a tandem bike—a bicycle-built-for-two. It's the perfect back-up plan. My decade old road bike was in the storage room, and all it needed was a tune-up at the local bicycle shop. I'll have Tom dig it out of its hiding place next weekend.

Contemplating my celestial observations after a decades-old comet left an impression on me was inspiring this morning. We all need a change of pace and the stars guide us in their own way. My shift began at ten o'clock and I had a bit of time to relax. With the couch pillow held close, I got into my calming zone, I turned on my essential oil diffuser. I inhaled the sweet lavender fragrance. This was my alone-time to daydream about anytime that surfaced inside me.

Toronto is home to 19th-century botanical gardens, in and around the heart of the city. Their centerpieces are tranquil Victorian glass solariums and ornate water fountains, with an abundance of manicured flowerbeds around the park grounds.

Year-round, I would find peace among the flowering native and exotic plants straining toward the sun. I'd watch innocent pollinators seduced by their aromatic nectar and alluring color. The spirit of the plants knew which species could do their bidding for them. It's one of Nature's naughty mysterious secrets.

I often used the memory of visiting one of my cherished park on sunny warm days to ground myself, and calm my nerves. It certainly helped to imagine the blue skies with its nurturing sun, and the fragrant blossoms in Allan Gardens, especially on a cold and gloomy morning. Baster leapt onto the couch and curled up by my side. The rhythmic splattering of raindrops on the window was soothing as my eyelids rested shut.

From an early age, I had the skill for floral design. My mother had a natural talent for growing an array of annuals and seasonal perennials, that created beautiful garden color schemes. But my craft was never good enough for the flower shop owner, Theresa.

She would insist on giving it her signature touch: a fancy ribbon added to a stunning floral arrangement. I would imagine Iris, the goddess of the rainbow, pouring a pitcher of her radiant healing waters over the flower shop to instill calm and peace. I visualized her shop as a heavenly oasis for nature's creations.

Baster walked over my legs and meowed in my face to bring me out of my reverie. I just had enough time to grab the umbrella from the kitchen and hustle over to the bus stop.

It's uncanny how she kept track of my schedule.

From Peru we moved to Australia, where the captain searched for his Alene. He learned that she had been forced to marry a white man who had taken a fancy to her, and had taken ship with him to England.

We moved on to London searching for Alene, but her trail grew cold. There was rumor of an Australian arriving with a Polynesian wife, but they were said to have boarded another ship soon after, as the Australian had been transported for capital crimes and must leave, or be executed. No one could tell us which ship they boarded next, or where to.

So, the captain settled in a city-square where he was gainfully employed by Lloyd's of London, helping them to assess the risk of proposed sea voyages. He gradually became restless, and his work suffered. He knew something was missing. It was his one true love Alene. I thought it was much like my own longing to reunite my dispersed fragments, in this other world. And perhaps we were both right?

Is not love the need for another to complete the self?

His employers could see he was not well, and so they retired him, and in recognition of his past excellent service, they gifted him a portrait of himself standing on the prow of his ship in a raging storm.

- CHAPTER 7 -
Toronto, spring 2022

The bus started pulling away from the curb. Drenched and chilled under my raincoat, I banged on the door in the morning rain. The bus jerked to a stop, and the driver looked disgruntled. He's probably behind schedule.

With a one, two, three count in my head, I hoisted myself up onto the bus, with a flash of my transit card at the reader. It was packed to its regulated capacity with the pungent smell of weathered clothes. My umbrella torn apart in the morning wind, jammed up against my leg as I cradled my oversized tote. I had squeezed into the last seat with a throbbing ankle from the sprint.

My eyes swept over a crowd self-absorbed with technology. They fidgeted with their devices, while juggling to hold their laptop bags, purses, and totes. The ride was bumpy with its erratic turns around the orange cones and barriers, that sometimes seemed to spontaneously self-create along the city streets.

The windshield wipers clicked back and forth. The breathy conversation mutters merged with the throb of the engine only to form a familiar gray soundscape.

I wiped the water drops off the screen, courtesy of my soaked hair. My finger scrolled down through the messages on my phone. I had begun to feel like the phone was becoming part of me. I am turning slowly into a cyborg, I admitted wryly. Then the phone rang as if it was listening to me. Do I answer? Can I ignored it? I was soon confronted with blank stares from those within earshot range, at my disregard for its sole purpose in life.

When it rang for a third time, I couldn't resist from the years of obedient behavior. I flicked the icon to accept the call. The name Iris flashed onto the dark screen. I squinted as it changed into a speckled screen. I slid further down into my seat. Intrigued, I watched the familiar zig-zag pattern of my star sign taking shape.

The constellation Aquarius was being mapped out for me on my screen. Weird, or what? Maybe, my parents tried to contact me from the other side? I've heard about these things. But, I was probably hacked with clever target advertising. Or, my phone was not OK after all.

Maybe the crash on the kitchen floor had damaged it more than I had thought. That's all I need ... another expense as the warranty ran out long ago. I'll have Tom reset the software tonight to see if that works. His star sign is Gemini, that makes him a pro with technology and communication devices.

A diverse mix of people step aboard with each stop, and most would spill out the backdoor at the subway station.

A stirring sauté of sizzling tension and resignation filled the aisle as phones lit up. A whirlwind of zipping sounds from incoming messages, with marital and business disputes were aired in public among strangers. It's part of the experience on public transit. I tried focusing on the windshield wipers to drown it out.

The noise grew louder and irritating. To keep out of others' affairs, I turned my hearing aid down and cupped my other ear. That's when I heard a soft tune. A poetic lyric that muted out the background noise. It sounded as if it was breezing through a faraway tunnel. I recognized the tune, so scintillating; so alluring....

But, where was it coming from?

When I was in the hospital after the loss of my parents, I had hummed this tune to myself in my medically induced coma daily, so the nurse recorded it on her phone. She played it back for me a few days before I was released. I did not know the song, though I suppose I could have heard it as a young child.

A raccoon parade strolled out in front of the speeding bus and the driver slammed on the brakes. The abrupt stop threw me from seated, up onto my feet. It broke my concentration of honing in on the tune's source. Spilled coffee rolled down the aisle's crevices. I skidded then ducked fast to avoid an unattended phone that was launched into the air.

The whooshing breeze skimmed by my cheek. It assured me that my life has been spared. I somehow latched onto the pole to brace myself, and wrenched my arm socket in a last survival attempt. It triggered a three-sixty vertigo whirlwind as I looked out the window with my speedy vision at the wobbly creatures meandering across the street at their own pace.

A sharp jabbing pain brought me out of my dizzy spell. This was my stop. My shoulders rolled down slowly as I raised my chin to stretch my neck before I moved. The driver apologized for the hard stop and lowered the step to meet the curb. My head jolted into a makeshift nod of thanks for getting me to work in one piece. I limped down onto the sidewalk.

The rain had lightened to a heavy Scotch mist—cold to the bone. I inspected the spokes that had pieced through the plaid nylon canopy. Looks like my umbrella has seen its last downpour. It's ready to retire into a recycle bin. At least I would make it by ten o'clock, even if its under overcast skies. Up went my trench coat's hood as the bus screeched away from the curb. It was only a short walk around the corner, and a few doors down on a one-way street to the flower shop.

The bus driver sped past with a blast of his horn. In a fast swerve, he knocked down a construction pylon to avoid a pedestrian running across the road on a red light with a phone glued to her ear. He shouted out the window pumping his arm furiously, but she didn't even look up.

Boxes of fresh cut flowers were stacked up on the doorstep. They were clearly visible but I still managed to trip over them, and my palms landed flush against the door. Water that had gathered in the awning, spilled over onto the cartons of roses, carnations, and daises. I lifted them out of the puddle and up onto my sore arm, then searched for the key in my tote.

The finicky keyhole challenged my other hand. There that's it, the reassuring, one-two click. I pushed the door open, shuffling inside sideways with the boxes. With my backside, I butted the door shut on my way to the cutting board, with the daily delivery. The table stood in front of a display cooler with its array of cut flowers, greenery, and floral arrangements.

With a long slow breath, I twisted my damp fallen hair up into a bun. My purse and coat had a designated spot in the backroom closet. My umbrella found refuge in the bin as I practiced my greeting in a whisper to myself.

With hands clasped together, I was ready to announce a cheery welcome. The door swung open on cue. The familiar heel click made my heart race. I never knew what kind of mood she might be in, but I was prepared for the worst with my rehearsed greeting moments earlier.

I called out triumphantly, how the flowers smell so fresh and doesn't it brighten up a dreary morning. But, Theresa walked past me in her usual abrupt manner. Without a word, she hung her coat up on her pedestal rack near the cooler. After an inconspicuous struggle to adjust her miniskirt, she sat down at the French leg desk. Legs crossed, she unlocked the drawer and powered-up her laptop. Chika, her fluffy white Bichon Frise, pranced onto his plush cushion beside her desk, with one paw hanging over the side.

"My front door opens at ten o'clock and closes after our last customer leaves even if it's after sunset. Has it ever crossed that feeble brain of yours to arrive early? Most of us do, if we want to get places in the world." Theresa spoke in a thick European accent. She pulled out a fancy e-cigarette.

Her words rang true as I tapped on my hearing aid's volume control. With a smile I adjusted it as I had turned it down in the bus. My hands soon rested on my hips as I planned my morning creation.

"You're on my clock!" Theresa snapped her fingers.

"It helps if I visualize the display."

"Make it happen! I don't pay you to fantasize. People grovel for work in this city. Make sure your bouquets match up with the laminated pictures displayed in the flip chart. Irene, flash reminder.... It's hanging on the cooler." Theresa blew scented smoke rings over her desk. Chika's eyes tracked them as his ears flopped over. "And Irene, wipe that blank look from your face before Cindy arrives. It's embarrasing for me."

I had started to work for Theresa a couple of months earlier, after I had started my shift at Khilto's. She was rude and demanded a lot. And she did a good job of it. I was tempted to quit but it was an ideal job for me. The few days a week worked into my schedule and all I had to do was avoid confrontation. I wanted to keep the peace and the income.

I only wished that she would change one day and act a little nicer. It had to be in her somewhere. I knew she had a tough life before she came to Canada. Theresa was a single mother, who had left an abusive marriage fifteen years ago, fleeing from her home across the ocean to escape. She had no one to lean on in this country.

Springtime, with religious holidays, weddings and graduations, was her busiest season after Valentine's Day and St. Patrick's Day. Then, there were corporate events and special orders for local residences. But, I've got to hand it to her, she was always on top of things. Despite her temperamental and unpredictable behavior, she was a good mentor for an aspiring entrepreneur in any sector that deals directly with the public.

"Irene, enough daydreaming read my lips!" She scrolled down the orders that came in overnight. Several private orders, plus a few requests from other florists to fill their own orders. She and a couple of other florists had formed a coalition to make each others' specialties, available to their customers in our delivery zones. It was good for everyone's business.

"Is Cindy's floral arrangement finished yet? She should be here soon. She's now a top event planner and it's her own bridal shower tomorrow. It's all over the Twitter-verse. Do I detect a hint of jealousy? Don't worry dear maybe someday you'll find true love, too."

"I haven't read about it, but will do."

"You know, Cindy used to have your job. That's right, she started here. She was a hard worker and good at it too, down to the last detail. She learned event planning from the ground up. I taught her everything she knows behind the scenes. She has ambition. Is it possible to cultivate this trait in yourself? This is your opportunity."

I decided to ignore these digs and instead fussed with the flowers and greenery fillers, then clipped a few more stems. A draft whistled through the cracked-open window as a perfumed breeze aroused my senses. I placed my hands on the worktable to steady myself. I was unable to recognize the odd scent around me as I peered outside. Birds swooped in to feed on the mist-covered ground and puddles. My eyes were drawn toward a dark moving swirl between two buildings.

It's as if it or whatever it was, caught my stare as my thoughts became saturated with the name Zephyr. It boomed into my head as I recalled a childhood memory of story time. He was a wind god in Greek mythology, and a companion of the goddess Iris.

Sharp words broke my distracted look.

"Earth calling, Irene!"

I rubbed down the goose-bumps on my arms.

"How's your love life? Tom is it? I've noticed that he never picks you up. Am I not right? Maybe he could drop you off so you're here by 9:45 AM. Now, surely he has noticed your limp? And, you on public transit?"

"We have different work schedules."

"Still, why doesn't he rearrange his? Ask him! Expect more and it'll happen, but it is your life, right, Irene? I sometimes wonder by your dreamy expression. Once you've finished the centerpiece, put some pizazz into this arrangement. It's for a surprise thirtieth birthday party." Theresa looked over the new order, and placed it on the worktable. "Oh, Irene, do something with that hair. You look like a floor mop." She rummaged through her desk drawer. "Take this, it's my hairdresser's card."

It is my life, isn't it? I thought. I slid the card into my pant pocket, with a nod of gratitude. Theresa swirled her chair around. Chika, in a glitzy-studded collar, jumped into her arms. I pictured Tom with maple syrup on his chin at breakfast earlier on. But it was what happened afterward that made me break into a warm smile. I'll ask Tom to pick me up after work. Why not? Then, Theresa could meet him and see what a wonderful man he is.

I turned around to unpack the rest of the roses. I couldn't confront her ritual inspection of my attire. So, with the long stem roses cradled safely in my arms, I proceeded to move toward the backroom where there was another workspace. It was complete with all the finishing touches: ribbons spindles, accent ornaments, and incredibly stylish vases. I quicken my pace toward the counter with an electric kettle and tabletop fridge.

With my next step, I was startled by a glimpse of my reflection in a full-length mirror at the end of the hallway. I turned fast for a second glance. The reflection that faced me was draped in an ancient robe trimmed in pearls, holding the flowers for Cindy's centerpiece in her arms. It is—or was it me? OMG! A laurel leaf wreath too? Had my childhood goddess-wannabe-wish come true?

Or, was it an illusion? A Freudian subconscious desire? I watched my reflection through rainbow clouds of misty precipitation as the particles condensed into huge water droplets. They rolled down the mirror, bounced along the hall, and splattered into puddles. The sight made me dizzy. I stumbled toward the glass. A footstool broke my fall and the flowers scattered around me. I struggled to catch my breath from the shock.

My head swerved to glance down the corridor. Theresa was nowhere in sight. I sat down on the stool. My ankle needed attention, as it had twisted awkwardly in the fall. I accepted the fact that I would never be as agile as before. But, I still wished my ankle would stabilize and strengthen. After my hallucinatory experience, I dreaded the thought that my head injury would haunt me forever too.

I removed my shoe and sock only to reveal a darkening bruised ankle. But anything is possible if you put your mind to it, I tried to assure myself. My eyes swelled up as I reached over to pick up the flowers.

"Why is that not in its proper place?"

I looked up to Theresa's voice as her stiletto tapped beside my shoe. "It's my ankle again, my foot gave out from under me." I dabbed my face with a tissue. "But not a stem broken or bent, every petal is still intact. See?"

There was a warm sensation stirring up inside me as I cradled my swollen foot in both hands. I focused on feeling better, doing better, being better. I closed my eyes and visualized. What would it be like if my ankle was better? Warmth flowed from hands and into my ankle. The swelling subsided instantly as my shoe slipped on with ease.

Then, another strange thing happened.

"You look overwhelmed, please don't get up, rest ... allow me." Theresa's tone changed from annoyed to concerned with outreached arms.

Taken aback by her actions, I placed the flowers into her arms and stood in from of the mirror. It's me, Irene Montgomery, in modern-day Toronto not during a Greek tragedy or in biblical times. Life would be quite boring and too predicable, if we didn't have an imagination.

"I appreciate your help, Theresa."

"No need to thank me, I'm always here for you." Together, Theresa and I arranged the flowers and greenery into the vase. The bells were hit by a gust of wind as the front door swung open. The sun had broken through the clouds. It cast a shaft of light into the room.

"Good morning beautiful people," a voice called out from the front room. "Anyone home? Knock-knock, ladies."

"Perfect timing, Cindy!" Theresa chimed in from down the hall. She waved her hand at me. It was her signal that I should greet Cindy in the front room as she gave the vase her signature touch: a red ribbon with silver trim. Theresa walked over with Chika prancing along at her heels. She placed the cellophane wrapped floral display in Cindy's arms.

"It's a stunning arrangement."

"Irene outdid herself again. She's the talented florist who replaced you. This is her own creation using a blend of color, fragrance, and alluring greenery. I'm astounded with her abilities. Irene was an answer to a prayer."

"And so you are as I can see," Cindy said as Theresa's face lit up enthusiastically.

"Irene, your hairstyle is simply lovely. Do let me know your stylist's secret." Theresa was thrilled to hear about my neighborhood salon. We made plans for an up-do and lunch next week. She insisted it was her treat in recognition of my dedication and skill.

We had many orders to fulfill before the delivery service arrived. It was a busy day and Theresa was terrific for a change. I saw a side to her that I never knew was possible. My ankle was clearly acting up that afternoon and I stumbled twice more, but it didn't bother me.

Had my wish come true? I didn't see this coming, but it was a wonderful surprise. It was as if my wish for kinder, gentler Theresa had come true. She had rolled up her sleeves to help me and sent me home in a taxi to put my foot up. Whatever magic spell was cast on her works for me. I hope she keeps it up.

The captain did not fare well and the strain for his yearning of what was, took a toll on his mental health. He became an eccentric recluse, which did not suit my purpose.

I helped him to find a clue, a hint, a rumor, of the Australian and Alene. A dockworker said he had seen a couple fitting their description stowing away one night on a ship trading from London to Halifax. He carried me with him to find her, packed in straw in a small chest, like a pirate's treasure.

He had brought a considerable wealth with him. But not long after we arrived in Halifax, he had suffered a raging fever from a disease brought over on a ship and in his delirium found himself in a fight with a sailor. He was robbed of his purse on the wharf.

All who met him thought he lost his mind afterward. He had to sell most of his belongings, and was soon destitute, In despair, he wandered the beaches and towns of the Province, searching for his lost love, whom he called his pearl. A treasure he would never again find in this life.

But I had use for his love, his longing. I trapped his energy, drop by drop, into his image in the portrait painting, every time he approached it in his room. When there was little of him left, he moved from the rooming house to charity. He *would beg for a meal and a bed for a night, or sleep in a doorway or a shed, even under the wharf.*

When the captain died, I was left in my box under the wharf beside him. I willed a storm wave to pick me up, and float me away. Caught in tossing waves, I fetched up weeks later on a rocky beach, sheltered by a point of land. I would need to bide my time, buried in the sand like a pirate's treasure, and perhaps that is not far off what I was? It was not far from Oak Island, where real treasure was buried.

The skills of lay mathematicians, architects, craftsmen, and laborers were crucial to that legend. The pirates built masterly chambers, and an intricate tunnel system with floodgates and rigged traps. Ingenious methods were taken to mislead any pillagers that might seek the buried treasure.

Legends of this treasure lent a mysterious allure to the entire coast, and no one could walk the beaches without wondering, if perhaps, here or there might be treasure, or way over there. But none came looking for me in the chest and years passed.

Zephyr blew the westerly wind, creating a gale. The waves of the North Atlantic battered the Nova Scotia shore, but Zephyr's target was below the water as the currents scoured mud and rock, excavating an overhang in an undersea cliff.

- CHAPTER 8 -

Nova Scotia, summer 1858

Clouds rolled over the rocky shore. The year was 1858, and at high tide, this point of land was an island in the Atlantic, off the shore of Nova Scotia. At low tide, it was connected to the mainland by a narrow pebble beach across which cattle and carts could be driven.

The cool ocean breeze played over a bed of clams in the sandy stretch between two cliffs. The waning waves from last night's gale served up pungent fish to the seagulls as hungry beaks and talons dove in. A lighthouse above the cliff across the small embayment, overlooked the rugged shoreline. The Thompson's were the light keepers. They lived in a three-room log cabin with an outhouse, and a fresh water river nearby.

It was a late summer afternoon. The Thompson children had finished their chores and home schooling. The three siblings took a narrow footpath through the field. They slipped under a splintered fence into the woods. It was not far to the low-tide isthmus. With the narrow strip of shoreline in view, they ran the last stretch to stand ankle deep in a quiet wave. Fred, the eldest, always took the lead with the wagon.

Their Mama had a strict rule. They had to return home before dark, or before the tide came in and cut them off, whichever came first. The children went to the beach one afternoon a week during the warmer months. Rain or shine didn't matter, their Mama knew children needed playtime.

Pearl alerted her siblings that the tide was turning. Fred rolled his eyes and watched on as her outcries never changed tune. Everything was either exciting or a warning of impending danger. She had turned ten this past spring and was more eager to build a sandcastle with her bucket and shovel than to dig for clams. With her shovel flippantly in the salty air, her delicate face was speckled with surf froth and sand.

Fred was comforted by a huge golden ball shrouded in wispy clouds as the salt stung his lips. It cast a lengthening shadow at his feet, telling him they had an hour or so, before they would have to head home.

The rush of waves snaked a cold path into the warm sand. It flowed into the widening hole as Pearl diligently cupped up the grainy landslide. Anna, the youngest, stomped out the excess with her feet. Both were meticulous and fast in their efforts against the ocean's onslaught.

With a flick and twist of the wrist, Pearl told her younger sister to make a stone dam to block the waves from their construction site. She was not allowed to participate in the delicate crafting of the castle, but was allowed to help in other ways.

At the tender age of five, Anna struggled to lift the big stones her sister's whim commanded. Tears welled up at her failure as her fingers failed to pry the stones off the beach. She always tried to please her big sister.

"It's my dungeon!" Pearl exclaimed proudly oblivious to Anna's tears. She calculated the castle's size with her hand as a ruler. A tangle of twigs jammed into the sand formed into a locked gate. She had read about Vikings and Normans in a picture book from the village library, and how fortresses were made.

Obediently, Anna propped up a piece of weathered wood as a drawbridge. Pearl hammered it in place with a stone as Anna picked out a wood sliver from her finger. She showed her sister the pinprick of blood, proud of having pulled out the sliver herself, and of being brave.

Pearl looked up as a rumbling sound that disturbed the air. A submarine cliff, undercut by the currents, had collapsed, generating the smallest of tsunamis. The current swept across the ocean floor. Pearl, Fred and Anna watched as the sea pulled out and a mounting wave came in, making them run for higher land, but not high enough to destroy anything except the sandcastle. Pearl started to cry.

"It's only a sand-castle!" Fred voiced his annoyance, with an eye roll. They built one each week and the ending was always the same. It'll be destroyed by the moonlit tide. So, what's the point? He was more interested in thinking about pretty girls with soft hair, and clothes that smelled of fresh bread. There was one in particular, but his friend Tom was probably going to beat him to her. He always did.

Fred pulled a basket from their wagon, and told Pearl to get the ragged towel that was under it. Their Mama had packed an afternoon snack. Sitting on the towel, he took out a bottle of water, and pried the cork out with his teeth like a man. The water was warm and it quenched his thirst. He passed the bottle to Anna. Pearl wandered at the surf-line, looking for shells or flotsam: washed up ship wreckage.

The seagulls voiced their territorial threats. They'd swoop in closer in hope of sandwich scraps. Their shrilling calls unnerved Fred as it always caught him off guard. Eagles and hawks could be seen circling higher up, waiting for the right moment to strike a seagull that might venture too far from the rest of the flock.

Pearl waved frantically for her sister. Anna marched over, shovel in hand. Pearl was standing over something sticking out of the sand, exposed by the monster wave. She was poking at it with a large stick. Anna soon joined her, and the two started digging around it in earnest.

"Papa says the tides wash everything ashore. That's if you can wait a lifetime or two." Fred hollered in earshot range. He pretended to be disinterested, but curiosity got the better of him. With toes flexed, he walked over the sharp sand and pebbles to see what his sisters were so excited about. An elbow shielded his wind-burned cheeks as he bent down, speechless.

It was a wooden chest bound in chains.

The children had grown up on stories of buried treasure. Not just the stories of Captain Kidd's treasure at Oak Island that everyone knew of. It was more than that. There were tales of other pirate treasures on these shores. Their Papa had books they were not allowed to look at. Mama was very strict. She said they were abominations in the sight of God that talked of other types of things: magical cups, books of spells, curses and such.

Mama made sure he kept those books far away from the bible stories and children's books, that she preferred they read. There were times, when she was not looking, Papa would show them pictures in some of these books. They were always more interesting than the bible stories, with their unrealistically well-behaved children.

But Mama also talked about treasures. She often reminisced about growing up in Halifax, where her mother had rented out rooms. One of the last renters Mama remembered, was a sailor, a man not quite right in the head though kindly. He talked to Mama when she was a little girl about the seafaring life and his adventures of the olden days, and of buried treasure.

This man was a famous treasure hunter in his day, she'd say. He was the captain of his own ship, and staked claim on a place called Oyster Secret. He traded the best pearls Europe had ever known, but was shipwrecked in a storm, and survived. When he came to Nova Scotia he was old with eyes that sparkled blue. He would take a boat over to Chester to spend time on the dock staring out to sea, and wandered the shores. Some said he was looking for a lost treasure he had buried here long ago. But his eyes told a different story. The captain was looking for his long-lost love. He could feel her presence pulling him, somewhere near the Village of Chester.

He disappeared one day. Some of his belongings were left behind in Grandma's backroom. Mama said she saw him down by the wharf a few months later in a dreadful state, but he did not recognize her. He was still searching. With these stories as their constant backdrop, it was no wonder that the box buried in the sand was clearly, in their minds a pirate treasure.

"Move aside, I'll deal with this!" Fred's voice cracked, almost deepening into his Papa's tone. He whacked a mosquito on his neck, smearing the blood into his palm. The birds cries had vanished between the cliffs. With the soft incoming whooshes on the shore's edge, his ear hovered over the fast sinking hole his sisters had dug.

A rumbling under the sand startled him. The pit's sides widened as the hole burst open with a bubbling sound. Frothy sludge fizzled up through the opening. A rush of putrid water followed, spouting up into his face.

Fred winced from the stench, angling his shoulder as his arm struggled to reach further down. With stretched fingers, he felt the underside of the chest. He got a hold of the thick chain and yanked hard but it hardly budged. Then it gave way with tremendous force.

The chest threw him over onto the ground, as it surfaced from the water pressure below that fountained out. Fred lay curled up and winded from the stomach blow. He panted heavily beside the chained box.

"It's an actual treasure. My dream came true!" Pearl was elated. She rubbed the ocean spray from her eyes. Anna giggled as her freckled cheeks lifted up into a smile. She twirled her ponytail around her finger, and hugged Pearl's waist. They turned to their brother and watched as Fred lifted himself up and onto his feet. Clearly shaken from the ordeal, he gave a yawn and a big stretch to show his sisters that he was fine.

On her knees in a torn skirt, Pearl turned to the chest. She started to chip away at the crusted barnacles with her shovel. Anna raced over and mimicked her moves with a stick.

"It's dangerous!" Fred warned. "A creature could be inside it. Maybe a poisonous sea urchin." One of the metal fasteners flung open as a rusted hinge snapped and fell to the ground. The chest jerked and settled back on the sand.

Fred raised a finger that rolled into a fist.

The girls jumped behind him.

Pearl exclaimed that it's alive.

Anna's eyes filled with tears.

"Big girls don't cry!" Fred voiced absently, his face glistening from sandy sweat. His muscles flexed, flinging the empty water bottle toward the chest. The glass cracked on the rusted lock and slid down into the rocky sand. With a firm hold, he tried to break the chain.

The girls chimed in for him to try harder....

They watched his hand sweep across the carved features of darted arrows that pointed to strange symbols over land and water. Fred palmed clean the images of the sun and moon with human faces. Fred knew this was special but only an ax would open it. It was rusted shut.

Fred looked up at the gray and red-streaked sky. He knew that they must leave before the water level rises over their path. He pictured Mama's worried face over the stove as she kept an eye on the open door, waiting for them to emerge from the woods across the field.

Fred didn't need to be convinced by his sisters. It was a treasure. He dragged the chest over to the wagon and heaved it on. One end at a time. He imagined his family's faces crowded around him as he broke the lock and chain. The top would burst open exploring gold coins. A rush of exuberance filled him with excitement. He had wished on a star for a better life and here it was.

Pearl's victory shone in her face. She threw a towel over his wind-scorched shoulders. Anna balanced the snack basket on top of the treasure as they made their way home. Fred took the lead, and Pearl pushed the wagon from the rear. The wheels rattled and rolled over the rocks, around the trees, and through the field. Anna skipped through the thorny shrubs that scratched her legs, but she didn't care. She was only excited to see her Mama's face beaming at her with love.

~~~

When a wheel spoke snagged on a stump, Fred struggled to free it. The wagon collapsed in front of their home, and the chest tumbled over.

They stood facing their Mama on the top doorstep as Peggy's scarfed head framed her scolding face that the children dreaded. In rolled-up sleeves, Peggy wiped her dry chapped hands on her apron. She eyed a storm rolling in over the lighthouse. The light behind the Fresnel lens needed a refill of whale oil, but with the children out of the house and Charlie sick in bed, she dared not climb the lighthouse ladder alone.

Ever since the night her husband had come home from the pub proud to have cleaned out a sailor, he was never the same. Charlie had lost the little real money they had that evening. He thought he had doubled their fortune as the sailor said it was real pirate treasure. But it was worthless gold-colored lead coins.

When he was sober the next morning and saw the junk on the table, he became a broken man and felt destitute inside. They still had the lighthouse as their duty, which they must keep up or be evicted from their cabin and gardens. Their lighthouse was often the only thing keeping the trading schooners out of Boston from wrecking themselves on the shallows and rocky headlands of the treacherous shore.

"It's late, you all know better than to make me worry. Fred! Get the laundry basket by the clothesline. Put it in the kitchen beside the stove and then follow me. Girls! Go in to your prayers then attend to your chores.

I must go up to the lighthouse. You are going to bed without supper. Why did you make me worry again?" Peggy wrapped a torn shawl around herself.

"Look Mama, it's because we found a treasure." The girls sang out and jumped around at her bare feet.

With barely a glance at the sand-crusted, seaweed-wrapped box, Peggy's shooing arms hollered out to never touch ocean trash. Under darkening skies, her backhand sheltered her eyes from the churning winds, with massive clouds overhead. Now it was all timing to do her paid job as her anguish was felt in her words.

The children did what they were told.

The chest was left outside.

A wheel on the red wagon spun in the rising wind.

The next morning, a sunrise rainbow arced over the lighthouse. And when the children bounced out of the cabin for a new day of adventures, the chest was gone.

I could feel the warm presence of the amulet around the figurehead in the atmosphere on the eastern shore. I had cajoled the captain, and the ocean, and the children to bring me here closer to the amulet.

The passage of timed decades has petrified my statue from wood, to stone, to something harder than stone. I was losing the ability to influence my surroundings, but the spark in the amulet near in the atmosphere keeps me aware.

I now had the power to move myself by other means, instead of depending on the inconstant waves and wind. I would then be able to find the third smallest fragment, and be whole again.

This fragment had entered a soul consciousness long ago. The human will be birthed under a future star array, ruled by my stardust energy, where I sought safe refuge in her future self.

But now was not the time.

Not wishing to become a child's plaything, I compelled Peggy in a sleepwalking dream to hide me in the cellar. There I could rest safe until the time was right.

The ripples continued to spread and they must spread further before the reunion of my parts could occur. Like a stone skipping across a pond, I must touch many more lives before returning to my sanctuary and companions in no-space beyond the rainbow.

Like ripples, human lives are much one like the other, all drawing from a common pool. Each life a ripple, the gods shape them, play with them, raise them up and dampen them down, all to meet the demands of their whims.

And like the ripples on the pond, their interactions make a fractal play of light as possibilities shadow and spread across the surface of time and space.

- CHAPTER 9 -

Toronto, spring 2022

Margie was five years Tom's senior. She had been his after-school and weekend sitter growing up, and insisted he call her his aunt. That was how he got to know her younger brother Fred. They were only a few months apart in age, and had become lifelong friends. From swing sets and sandboxes to midnight movies in sleeping bags with popcorn, Margie had been a major stabilizing influence in Tom's life and was his confidant.

Margie had sent him a white glove invitation hand-delivered to his hotel for her antique store's grand opening gala. The day had finally arrived in mid-March. Margie heard the familiar bells tinkle as Tom entered the front door. She rushed over with a flute of a fruity-bubbly for him. They clinked glasses to celebrate.

"You really outdid yourself!" Tom leaned over to scoop up a couple of canapés from a sterling silver tray.

"Delicious isn't it? I'm thrilled you took timeout from work this afternoon. What's with the awkward pose?"

"Well, feeling a little stiff in the wrong places. Irene had persuaded me to join her at her fitness studio. Big mistake, I haven't been quite right ever since. There's always a first and last time for everything."

Marge laughed brightly with an awkward hip swirl. "I've never been particularly flexible either. You'll feel better soon. Why didn't you bring her with you?"

"Irene is at work. She has an affinity with Nature and masquerades as a primeval florist in her other part-time world. She says it's innate in her." Tom rubbed his neck.

"That sounds like Irene! She drawn to those invisible flower mystics. You know, the spiritual forces behind Nature. She told me about them at Khilto's. She had researched this concept in depth. I can imagine her picking Lilies and Bulrushes in the Nile. Such a silly thought, isn't it? Now, follow me, I have a surprise." With interlocked arms, they walked by the other guests that milled around admiring the antiques on display.

Margie's office was painted in burnt umber with original hardwood floors. On a polished table stood a blue and gold Venetian vase, with long stem roses from Fred. Tom was drawn to the portrait on the wall.

"That's incredible!"

"Isn't it?" Margie picked up her ebony magnifying glass from the table. "It's safe to come closer. They've been lost at sea since 1835. Look at this brass plaque at the bottom."

"Margie, there's something timeless about this."

"The captain was a brave man by the look in this woman's eyes. I have a hunch they'll never be forgotten."

~~~~~

"It was a different world in the good old days."

"Tom, it's only how you perceive it I suppose. But, love never changes and whatever the story of their love was, the same story could have played out endless times over the centuries with different undying themes."

They chatted and analyzed the portrait in detail. Margie had compared it with other portraits from this era through museum databases and private collections. Both speculated about the mystery couple and the artist. They both agreed it had a peculiar quality about it.

"Oh, I have something for you, I almost forgot." Margie bent over to fiddle with the key that unlocked the desk. "I placed it in this drawer the other day."

Margie's hand rummaged around in a mess of chandelier crystals, charms and broken pocket watches. "There are plenty of ancient relic and coin necklaces for sale in the showcase up front, but this one is special. It had your name on it. That's odd. It had managed to move to the far end of the drawer." Margie lifted out the piece and jiggled the wooden drawer in.

"The face looks so real!" Tom let her drop it into his palm as his thumb touched the exquisite features of a sun-face. It was carved into a round stone with a crystal in her brow that sparkled blue. The piece was set into a bronze shell case with hieroglyphs.

"That's an incredible artifact, valuable?"

Margie wore a red lipstick puckered look as her head bobbed around in thought. "It's probably a forged replica of an old relic. My appraiser says the metal is bronze, and the face is carved into carnelian, but the small stones he could not identify. He thought they might be from a meteorite because of their blue glow. I said that whoever had made it was able to lasso a shooting star, because that's what meteors are made of."

Tom looked closely at the amulet.

"Anyway, tarnished bronze works for me. It sounds better than any old metal. Or maybe the stones are only glass who knows. The appraiser didn't want to disappoint me. Anyway, he knew it was a gift and didn't need an official appraisal. Everything else has a price tag except this piece. It's such an exquisite find though, isn't it? To me, this amulet is priceless."

"Well, it's certainly striking. It's extraordinary for an ancient-looking replica if that's the case."

"I've taken some pictures to research it on the web, to be sure. This was also one of the last mysterious items I found during the renovation and clean-up. I dug it up in the basement." Margie stomped on her chunky heels.

"I mean literally! I had to excavate it with my hands I found it in the basement only hours before the contractors showed up to lower the floor. This amulet was buried in the earthen clay floor, jammed under a weather-beaten cabinet. It was only a link of the chain glinting in the flashlight beam that caught my eye. I had to pound out a panel of rotting wood to dig it up. It was an odd discovery, like the Ouija board that you found under the stairwell."

~~~

"Really?" Tom sank into the armchair opposite her.

"Yes, and oh, the dust that came down with each blow of my pry bar made a mess of my hair. I was blanketed in a cloud of some kind of old vermiculite insulation. I just hope there wasn't any asbestos in it. The wood finally splintered and freed this beauty." Margie reflected on that moment. "You know, amulets or any spellbound relic are only found if they want to be—and by whom. Isn't it incredible that you were its chosen one?"

Tom was touched by her gesture and her interesting take on the discovery. Margie meant a lot to him, especially during this challenging time.

"I've cherished our friendship over the years, please allow me." She placed the chain over his head with the amulet's face pointing forward, at heart level. "Prominent people and rulers wore jewelry to show their power and notability. Oh, look what you've done … I've got goose-bumps all over my arms. You were meant to wear this amulet." Margie saw his hesitancy in his posture. He stood up to stretch his legs.

"It's also useful during a midlife crisis. You'll get through it, with Irene by your side. See this as a protective shield." Margie touched his cheek and his face relaxed.

"OK, I got the message. Now let the magic begin." Tom rubbed the amulet on his sleeve as if it were a magic lamp. "Done! I made a wish to the good mystic inside."

"And your wish?"

"It's a secret or it won't come true. My lips are sealed."

Tom rested his arm across her shoulder as she chuckled softly at his joke. They walked past the basement door. Margie rattled the handle to make sure it was locked. It was fully renovated with proper air vents and a backflow prevention valve. The floor was lowered and tiled, and the wall panels were replaced. It was a private storeroom where she could do minor repairs to small items.

The prospective buyers, mainly interior decorators were impressed with the antiquities, both large and small, for possible clients. They mingled under the chandeliers as the light shone on the polished furniture and danced upon the silver tea sets and tableware.

Servers in vintage clothing navigated through the room with trays of canapés and champagne spritzers. The clerk was busy ringing up grand opening sales as orange sold stickers were placed on the pieces that would be leaving the premise later that day or delivered.

Tom caught a glimpse of himself in a beveled mirror in the far corner. He took a step back struck by swirling ripples over his reflection. The luminous halo vanished as Margie glanced over at him through the crowd.

Tom met up with Fred later that week, at their regular lunch spot: Malcolm's diner near his office building. Tom fidgeted in his seat with his fleeting thoughts.

"I helped your sister with a final inspection of the basement last month before the opening. We cleared out a few more things before the contractors signed-off on their work. It's an old building and lots can be hidden behind the walls and under the floorboards. It's best to check before it's sealed up for another century."

"Better you than me. I heard about the amulet."

"A good luck charm that's all it is. Oh, Margie sure has business smarts. It runs in your family."

"For generations now, it's part of our family heritage." Fred tucked a napkin into his shirt collar as the server maneuvered her way around to their table.

"Two daily specials for my favorite patrons: Malcolm's clubhouse sandwiches, hand-cut fries, and a coke for you." Fred removed the toothpicks from his sandwich that kept it stacked high. He put them beside his dish as they always come in useful after lunch.

"Margie's grand opening turned into an afternoon street party under blue skies." Tom shook the ketchup bottle until it spurted out onto his fries. "There was a parade of white-gloved servers. Everything on display was for sale. She even had discreet price tags on the silver trays they used to serve the libations."

"I heard that they all sold too."

"By the time I arrived you had already left. I heard you had to pick up Sally. Did you check out the black cylinder-style top hat filled with embroidered face masks? They were leftovers from your sister's holiday gathering last year. The vintage hat was at the front door on a stand. Margie sure knows how to make people feel comfortable in her store."

Fred chuckled thinking about the display. "Curiously enough, the name Casper, was stitched along the underside of the hat's rim. It was eyed over by all the guests. You couldn't miss it. Casper was probably a wealthy gentleman, or an educated bachelor that charmed the ladies. Anyway it was another 19th-century surprise discovery for my sister. She found it in the attic along with his engraved cigar box."

"Maybe he was a gigolo?"

"Oh, what I'd give to have lived in that era."

"Count me in too, Fred—I'm there. Anyway, Margie unraveled yet another piece of history—a silk carpet runner. She had it rolled out on the sidewalk. It was found in the basement stuffed behind an old coal-burning furnace. The dry cleaners took extra care with its restoration, as red is a hard color to revive. By invitation only? Now, that was a damn good move. The word got around fast. The neighbors gathered on the corner as they tried to get a glimpse inside." Tom put down his water glass as Fred leaned in, both elbows on the table.

"A captain has captivated my sister's attention."

"Margie showed me the portrait with his love in his arms. The seaman's eyes looked conniving to me like he was planning an escape. I'm sure he's eager to break out, he was framed." Tom tried to be witty. "There's a myth that a few portrait painters of that era knew the secret of how to trap the soul of the sitter. Imagine being held captive by strokes of oil paint, then sealed in with a layer of varnish. Margie told me all about it."

~~~~~

"My sister said that?" Fred gulped down his coke.

"And she went on to say it's in the last brushstroke that catches the twinkle of life. That's when the artist knew it was finished. The soul was trapped inside it. Not all of them signed their work, either. Margie suspects it was to conceal the mystic painter's identity into secrecy, for obvious reasons in that era."

"What was the magic stroke?"

"When moonlight is angled at 90-degrees onto the eyes and when the star sign Gemini is brightest, specks of paint and crystal dust are flecked onto the irises. Then, far into the future as the Zodiac wheel rotates in the heavens to a specific time, a doorway opens for the soul to re-enter into this world. But, it will remain invisible until it finds a body to possess." Tom shuffled in his seat as he recalled what Margie had told him. The antique store had much more of an effect on her than he first realized.

"What's gotten into my sister?"

"Who knows but she's convincing."

"No one is captive in her store."

"I have to admit, Margie's gone a little overboard trying to figure out this couple."

"Anyway, how's things with Irene?"

Tom told Fred about the side-plank incident, and Fred, remembering his own experience with Sally, commiserated.

∽∽∽

I awaited the return to my sanctuary outside this mortal plane. Fellow deities Zephyr and Bastet were also touching this world, seeking to bend time and events, to guide the flight of my three fragments, making it so those skipping stones would touch the surface at the right places, leave the right ripples, and not sink forever into oblivion.

I know the events that have been set in motion, will soon make me whole again. It's only the flow of earthly time that keeps me waiting. Ripples continue to spread, some weaker, some stronger, but all are linked and interacting to form a complex dance of light on the water of this world.

I see the reflection from a far ripple: I am in the atmosphere of an autumn breeze in a park, in Toronto, in the year 1925. I watch as an old woman tosses nuts from a paper bag onto the grass. She is feeding the squirrels.

I know she is connected to me, and I to her.

My sight follows her home, feeling the rightness of where she goes, of being with her.

〜〜〜

- CHAPTER 10 -
Toronto, autumn 1925

I tossed the last peanut out of the bag, watching as a squirrel snatched it off the grass and bounced toward the nearest tree. My tree, I felt, as my initials could still be read where an old flame had carved them in the bark with an apple knife. It feels like it was only yesterday.

This morning's storm left behind a luminous rainbow. Its iridescent hues were breathtaking over the autumn leaves. I've never seen anything quite so brilliant, but my afternoon stroll in the park had left me feeling distant for some reason. When I got home, I stepped over to the calendar hanging in the breakfast room and crossed off this day: October 5, 1925.

I threw a log into the cast iron stove in the kitchen. A water kettle simmered on top of it. Who needs one of those fancy electric stoves that will stop working when you most need it? They're only a fad along with all the other 20th-century inventions.

My name is Mrs. Karmen.

I live in a Victorian red brick house with fancy gingerbread woodwork scrolling around the eves, and the most exquisite stained-glass windows on the street. It still has the original bay windows that my father built himself, and ornately carved whitewashed porch bannisters. A coat of paint is all it needs to bring it back into its glory. It's a massive home for one person.

To help pay for the upkeep, I used to rent out rooms to working–class men and young women. Now, at seventy-seven this January, I'm still healthy and curious, and though I try not to think of myself as a number on a life scale, I know my time is fast fading.

I've aged gracefully and still have my wits about me, but that does not impress the authorities. I am an old woman living alone with a debt to pay. A notice was nailed to my front door weeks ago, advising me that this house was being seized by the city for the back taxes owing on the property. Who knew that property taxes had to be paid? When he lived, my father took care of such things. Since then, well, I guess after a few decades, even a city gets tired of waiting for what they are owed.

The city will take possession of the house. The contents will be auctioned off next week. Everything is still mine to sell up until the last day. The auctioneer will be here tomorrow to start the formal cataloging. A few pieces I will take with me, and a few more of the finer things, I'll sell on consignment at the antique store up the street.

Whatever is left here, the city will sell with the house for the back taxes. If the proceeds exceed the amount owing, they will give the excess to me, but my lawyer has told me not to expect much. Those in charge do not try very hard. I will go to live in a rooming house. I will now know that life from the other side. I will be a good guest I suppose ... not too demanding and will keep to myself.

Although they'll no longer belong to me, I've sheeted the sofas and chairs and locked up most of the rooms. It was that last turn of a key on the second floor that kindled a memory of my secret room in the upper attic. I haven't set foot in there since I was in my forties. It was a place close to my heart, but after I stumbled on the steep, winding stairs one day, I became afraid to climb it again.

The stairwell was only accessible from the pantry off the kitchen on the main floor. But as I would soon lose the house, my last chance to revisit that old once-familiar and comfortable space would soon be past.

I've no siblings anymore, nor children, and remained a spinster-widow in this house after my true love disappeared during a storm on the Gulf of St. Lawrence. My outlook on life changed the night he vanished. This house is all that remains of my family's legacy. It was built during the last century. So says the carved cornerstone hidden behind the mailbox. It has become hard to see screened by Pye weed and dandelions. Jarvis Street is home in Toronto, with its backdrop of churches, recreational pavilions, and horticultural gardens.

I'm not far from the lake, though it seems every year the city expands further away. The lake is filled in with buckets of rocks. Maybe one day there will be no lake left. People will be able to walk to the Toronto Islands. The city continues to grow upward and outward with newcomers, arriving by the railway.

The silk drapes moved in the breeze that stirred up the scent of mothballs from the clothes stacked on the floor. I had begun going through my closets several weeks ago, sorting through the memories to select those few items I would take with me.

I noticed something strange for this time of year. It was only autumn, yet frost patterns had formed on the windowpane. It made me wonder if the crystal shapes are imprints of Nature's patterns that guide all living things?

My un-religious belief in the power of Nature was from my father. He was a Freemason and studied its mysteries. A floor-to-ceiling bookshelf had stories of the occult, mythology, and natural philosophy. There was a separate oak shelf in the far corner for the bible and religious relics. Father honored my mother's request.

The glass fogged up as my breath quickened in an attempt to erase its history that never really disappears, it only transforms into something else, father would say. I drew PK, my initials, in the condensation. My finger chiseled off the thin layer of frost around the outer edges to frame it. Tired from my excursion to the park, I walked over to the couch to rest under the bay window. My embroidered pillow against my chest comforted me.

The younger generation doesn't understand how difficult it is to be old and alone and adapt to change.

I thought about this house and my life here, with the terrible tragedies as well as the touching moments. I would be leaving this house, and it deserved to have its history remembered before I left.

I let myself slip into a reverie.

My father had survived the Atlantic crossing from Liverpool to the New World. It took weeks on an overcrowded vessel that had the cheapest tickets. People were packed into the bottom deck with unsanitary conditions and little food and water. Many malnourished passengers died from illnesses and were thrown overboard. Others went delirious from high fevers, while some choose to jump over the rails to end their suffering. The ship had landed on the eastern coast of Nova Scotia long before Confederation.

Father was one of the fortunate ones that had survived, though he endured lifelong illnesses from the journey. As children, we grew up in the small out port of Chester, near Halifax. When I was young, father was a gambler with a wandering eye. Handsome, he was tempted into the sin of adultery. I think that pushed mother closer to God. But he reformed from threats of losing his family. Then after Nova Scotia joined with the other Provinces to form the Dominion of Canada, and my siblings and me were on our own, he and mother moved west.

By that time, I had married and my husband was Tom Karmen. Five years my senior, he was my brother Fred's best friend, and a hardworking man from a good family.

Tom and his father built us a house nearby. It was small but comfortable, with room for children, and an outhouse in the backyard. But as First Mate on a cargo ship that worked the route from Halifax to the center of the new country's wealth, Montreal, Tom was rarely home, and children did not come. Dreaded loneliness filled me with sorrow.

My parents traveled the railway to Toronto, where father kept the account books for a coal delivery company. The office work suited his fragile health better than had farming or lighthouse tending. He was smart and worked his way up over the years. He also received an inheritance from his brother, who had died in a railway accident in Halifax, and bought this fine house.

Mother died from diphtheria shortly after they arrived in Toronto. I still visit her grave marker in Mount Pleasant Cemetery, under a magnificent tree that had been a small sapling when mother was buried there. Purple wildflowers blossomed around her in springtime.

One day, only two years after my parents went west and just over one year since mother died, my beloved Tom disappeared. He loved being on the water. The maple leaves were in their golden red glory that autumn day. Squirrels were busy preparing their nests in the branches and neighboring rooftops, with winter stashes buried in the front yard of our Halifax home.

Tom had taken ship a few days earlier, on a routine cargo run up to Montreal. He was on a vessel called the Khilto's, due back the next day. He found solace and peace out on the ocean and in the Gulf of St. Lawrence. It was his place to clear his mind and wash away his worries in the moving tides. Tom would always throw a copper penny into the water as an offering for safe passage.

From my porch, I saw storm clouds move in over the lake with incredible speed. The southerly winds forcefully blew me up on my toes. I made it inside. But, it took great effort to close the front door. From the window, I watched the skies turn pitch black, etched with electrical flashes. The harbor lit up under the thunderous bolts that unearthed me. The weather had only called for a hazy overcast. The storm came out of nowhere and with a fury. It lasted nearly three days.

The other boats all made it back safely to the docks, or found other harbors close by. But Tom's ship did not come home that day, or the next day, or the day after that. The community searched for days up and down the river in the Gulf, and on the eastern shore. But they found nothing. Weeks later, we heard the news.

The Khilto had washed up, with no sign of violence, but with no one aboard. It was reported as an abandoned ghost ship. And most strangely, it washed up on the shores of Toronto, wedging its bow into the rocks near an old warehouse, a log cabin really, that had once been a fortified trading post. The newspapers of the day, more interested in lurid prose to attract readers than in the truth, speculated that a mysterious force was bringing the cargo to the trading post.

~~~~

The authorities did eventually move the cargo to the warehouse's basement, where it was piled into the warren of tunnels underneath the warehouse that dated from its use as a gunpowder magazine during the War of 1812. But, with the mystery of the missing crew and the ship being hundreds of miles upstream of Montreal, where it had been supposed to make port, Lloyd's of London refused to pay out on the insurance. The cargo was sold at auction for pennies on the dollar.

Tom was gone and in those days, there was no help for a twenty-year-old, childless widow of a First Mate. Though my in-laws were kind, I could not live with them, and they could not afford to support me in my own house. So, I moved to Toronto to live with my father, and perhaps in some way to be closer to the mystery of Tom's disappearance and his ghost ship.

It was only six years later that a milk truck struck my father before sunrise. Startled, the horse reared from a dog bolting out under its hoofs. Milk-trays toppled as bottles smashed on the macadam-surfaced road, and racks of eggs were splattered across the street. His scream made me jump out of bed and run to the window.

Remembering the horrific scene still makes me shudder. My father's legs were sprawled out from under the wheels. People had gathered around him, pointing and shouting. The housekeeper ran into my room to close my window shutters but it was too late, I saw everything.

The shrilling of the police whistles and clanging of the ambulance bells pierced throughout the streets, and stopped outside our house. I hung out my window and screamed frantically as I watched him being carried away on a stretcher. The coroner said that he died instantly and did not suffer.

After his Will was settled and the tax collector and creditors took their share, I was left with only the house. It was a full-time job to manage, and I needed the funds to pay the gardener and the live-in housekeeper, who were almost family retainers. So, I rented out rooms to pay for their upkeep and my own.

I invested the little extra I had each month at Woodbine Race Course, by the shores of Lake Ontario. I suppose it was an inbred passion, a legacy of my father's gambling days when I was a child. But unlike him I was good at it, or at least lucky I suppose. I made more than I lost and was able to keep a decent lifestyle.

My friends and I dressed in high fashion. We would always wear ornate hats to impress each other at the races. And our gentlemen friends wore their tailored jackets and sporty caps.

I had a few suitors, but only one was serious after my late husband, Tom. We spent a lot of time at the race course in the club's dining room decorated with sterling silver trophy plates. His private table had a spectacular view overlooking the track. Casper was years younger than me, an ambitious young man, swanky in his demeanor.

Casper seemed determined to live the high life at all costs, and always showed me respect and gratitude. With a hat tip greeting and a smooth nicety, he charmed the widows and maids into giggles and gossip.

He helped me buy a thoroughbred racehorse of my own, and I named her Mabel's Brizo. She were boarded and ran at Woodbine Race Course. She placed in the top three finishers one year. And, they're off, my friends and I would shout in chorus as I recalled the horses breaking out of the starting gate, with a snort and a full-rein tease by the jockey. A few years later, having lost a few bets and sadly, Casper too.... I had to sell her.

I was quite the Gibson Girl in those days. The feminine ideal, always on top of the latest trends. From closely following the gossip about the wars in Europe to the affairs of Queen Victoria and her royal brood, to messing about with séances, Ouija boards and mesmerism. I was among the first on my block to own an Edison Phonograph, and one of the first subscribers to the telephone exchange—a made-in-Toronto toy.

I was always on top of the trends when I was young. But as I got older, I found it harder to stay current, and was less interesting. I went from playing Cribbage with my friends to quiet evenings with my needlepoint.

My gardener had found a more prestigious employer with spectacular seasonal gardens, and deeper pockets. So, before he left, I had him take out some flowerbeds and put in more lawn to simplify the upkeep. The housekeeper had to leave soon after, to care for her aging sister. Without their help, I reduced the number of boarders I took in, and reduced their rent if they did work around the house that I could not do myself.

I was among the last to electrify my house after the first world war. With an avant-garde mix of Victorian and Edwardian furnishings, my wallpaper and drapery was still stuck in the 1800s. The expense of redecorating was no longer an option. I had sold most of my artwork and jewelry when my income plateaued. The glamorous lifestyle investment finally paid off much later in life, which I am grateful for now. My last boarder was a University College student. She studied English literature under this roof. Her room was sheeted and locked up long ago.

The brass knocker pounded hard on the door, startling me out of my meandering thoughts as I bolted upright. I dared not open the door to invite another conversation with a city official. What was the point? The end result wasn't going to change. From behind the curtain, I watched the inspector place another notice under the knocker. He adjusted his cap and walked briskly away in his shiny boots.

Obviously the inspector was only doing his duty. Young with no remorse in his demeanor, he wanted to ensure that I had received all the notices. Or, if I had not received them, that they had at least been delivered, which was the same thing in the eyes of the law.

I looked up the street to the corner store's calligraphed awning: Gora's House of Antiques. It was a family run business. They had sold many of my things since they opened a few years ago. I would take a few items there from time to time to pay some bills.

There had been quite a commotion there a few days ago. I had stepped out on the porch and called to my neighbor to see if she knew what the fuss was about. She said that it seemed someone had stolen an automobile. The owner was raising a huge ruckus, demanding the police arrest everyone in sight.

The ripples intersect and become confused. Is there really a difference between one ripple and the next? Are ripples all the same, or are they infinitely different, like snowflakes? I think infinitely different, but as feathery ice crystals in all their variety all have six points, all the ripples I have created share some common features in their rainbow refractions cast upon the mortal world.

Zephyr and Bastet reinforce this, meddling as they do to subtly guide the reflections to the highest climactic point that fate has decreed. I see the intrinsic patterns of the ripples all at once, though to one standing in the trough of a ripple, I suppose that one valley of water is all they would know, all they would see from this angle.

I move my attention to another ripple.

- CHAPTER 11 -
Nova Scotia, autumn 1925

At the height of dramatic change, in the Roaring Twenties and the Jazz Age, a red automobile motored on with speedy motion on a road, along the Nova Scotia shore. It was a Gray-Dort Special Touring Model, produced by a Canadian automaker in Chatham, Ontario, and stolen by its occupants ten days earlier.

Tom, a skinny teenage delinquent, jerked the clutch. In the passenger seat was his uncle Fred, out on a jailbreak. They had pinched the gasoline-powered, six-cylinder engine motorcar outside Gora's House of Antiques on Jarvis Street in Toronto, where a crowd had clustered together. Luxurious and touring automobiles were becoming more common, but only the wealthy could afford them.

It was early afternoon on October 15, 1925.

The Village of Chester stretched alongside the newly macadamized highway. Its vastness lingered far into the distance. Tom drove toward the trail of blackened soot in the sky that poured from the chimneys of the lumber kilns. This was a bustling coastal site for commerce and trade. Lumber, fishing, shipping and shipbuilding were industries that thrived on the shorelines where the dockyards connected the old and new worlds.

Fred had never seen the ocean before three days ago. He couldn't get enough of the infinitely varied cloudscapes on the horizon, like the wheat fields on the prairies only more vaster. The seagulls' cries and swoops startled him for hours, upsetting his stomach.

Tom's eyes were focused steadily on the road.

A huge masthead appeared out of nowhere as a shipwreck rose out of the ocean. Fred swung around to his right for a second look, squinting into the blaring sun. It was far out from the rocky shore with its reflection upon the waters. The illusion submerged leaving a telltale rippling whirlpool as a luminous halo formed with a finger over her lips. The startling face was blown onto the glass windshield before vanishing.

"That mince pie, chowder, and ginger ale are making me see things. Oh, queasy is coming on too." Fred's chin was protruding out from the torn and stained button-down shirt collar as he belched loudly with relief. He pressed his palms into his stomach to settle it down.

Tom's worn down shoe pumped on the foot pedal. The automobile puttered then jolted to a stop. The gasoline tank was empty by the choking sound of the engine. He clutched the steering wheel. Fred was thrown forward in the reddish-brown leather seat. With his hands on the dashboard, he pushed himself upright.

~~~~~~

"Is that the signal, we're there?"

"Looks like this is the end of the road for this motorcar." Tom's hands raked nervously through his thick curls. He stepped out of the car to stretch his legs. He gave the automobile an elbow polish. "It sure shines red with money though."

Fred's hand moved from his head onto the door. "Well, it sure has good power and speed too. It's nicer on this side of the bars, but easy does it on the breaks. Since you broke me out of jail, I realize I'm not what I used to be."

Tom's foot kicked up a dust cloud. He spit out the chewing tobacco onto the ground. Fred stumbled out of the car onto the deserted stretch of road, cows mooing in the distance. He unbuttoned his trousers and relieved himself by the side of the road.

"Leaving a territorial mark, partner?"

Fred's eye twitched. "What did you call me?"

"Sorry partner, err, I mean, uncle Fred. It was an honest slip-up. We sure fooled them men of the law two weeks ago. Those Winnipeg jailers must be dumbfounded. And we're long gone."

"I want you to understand something. I was innocent. Oh, I am not innocent anymore: jail break, car theft, and lots of other petty crimes. But that all came after I was wrongly accused. I was sent to jail for a theft I did not commit. Jailed for living with a woman of Métis heritage and not for anything I've done wrong."

"I heard about it on the streets."

"And it was in jail that I had to become a crook. It was the only way to survive in there. It is a hellhole, and it makes good people bad. I used to be good in Winnipeg and my mother would have been proud. You know, so none of this partners-in-crime stuff, hear me? We'll find this treasure and there will be no more crime for either of us. We'll each find ourselves a good woman and become honest upstanding citizens."

But, Tom yearned for a life of adventure. He was not ready to settle down. He had just turned four when his mother had abandoned him, and a neighbor took him in off the streets.

"We've had nothing but good luck for a while now. You broke me out. We jumped a train with a cargo of grain. It was a good place to rest our heads. At the stop in Thunder Bay, Ontario, where they were loading the grain into the elevator for shipping it east across the lakes. I lifted some mark's wallet with enough green in it to buy us passage on a steamer headed for Detroit."

"You did good there."

"There we hitched a train to Toronto where we stole this automobile. Now, there's no way the coppers have followed that trail. Out here I'm a free man. No one has ever heard of me and my private business is mine alone. Luck has been with us every step of the way, but we can't get sloppy. It's luck that it has been not good planning .... And, luck runs out sooner or later."

Tom turned nineteen not long ago and had left school as soon as he hit the double digits. Since then he managed to survive as a farm hand. There was crop and fence work in summers and cattle work year-round. These were paying jobs. It gave him a place to hang his hat in a barn or on a haystack. Sometimes he had a bed for a night to observe a world different from the Winnipeg slum he had grown up in.

But, Tom had grown restless as young men sometimes do. So, he conceived the scheme to break his only uncle out of jail and go on the run with him.

"Looks like the spare gas fuel can is empty too."

"Boy! Give me a hand! Time to cover up our trail. We'll find a gas pump after we get what we came for." Together, they pushed the automobile off the pebbled side road and into the brush behind the bushes. It was not far from the Village of Chester's welcome sign.

Fred took out a folded paper from his pocket. "According to this map, the buried treasure should be down this road close to a water tower. I believe that's it way over there. My cellmate had found himself in a bad place with bunch of toughs in a poker game. So, he stashed the box in the basement of a general store where he was hiding. It was around twenty years ago. Said he was going to die in jail, as the consumption disease was taking him one day at a time. And, he liked me enough to give me the secret. He must've felt I would break out sooner or later. It's time we get a move on. We're almost there."

～～～

It was a strenuous mile walk, but they made it in good time. Tom scratched his head as Fred's jaw dropped. They could hardly believe their eyes. The sight stopped them in their tracks. It was a bustling place of commerce and activity with a decorated running fountain.

"The paper says the general store is not far from the main crossroad. This must be it." Fred looked up at a shingle hanging from an awning across the street. They zigzagged through busy traffic, then stepped up onto the whitewashed porch. Fred's eyes went wide at the elaborate window display, and a poster nailed to a side post caught Tom's eye. He was revved up. Living a life of danger excited him.

"Hey, there's a carnival, with games and prizes."

"Boy, no need to overstay our welcome. This is the place, all right, we're just in-and-out. Got it?"

On either side of the door was a smoking bench.

The door swung open with a jingle.

Fred cleared his throat, muttering through his fingers. "Watch my moves, follow close." With a snappy hand signal, they made their way into the store, where a bead board counter stood to their left, in front of narrow aisles lined with shelves stocked ceiling high, with handy tools. Straight ahead was a room with barrels and shelves of foodstuffs, to the right was a marble counter with a soda fountain and a row of shiny stools. A menu on a side mirror listed the flavored syrups and ice cream.

Further down the main aisle was an adjacent room, with furniture and dishes and other household goods. A sign pointed to a narrow and steep staircase, advertising clothing and footwear for the whole family on the upper floor. The creaking wood planks told of the proprietor's location as a lanky man poked his head around a stack of shovels to greet them.

"Haven't seen you before. A wave washed you in?" The shopkeeper leaned his broom up against the wall. He tugged his vest down fashionably, then ran his fingers through his silver hair. He was prepared for business.

"Just passing through.... We need a few things." Fred tried to act sophisticated. He pulled his pants higher up, and tugged down his button-popped shirt.

"On the road before dark!" Tom assured him.

"So, what can I do for you, gents? Tobacco, cigars, cola?" With a pencil and writing pad in hand, he licked a finger and flipped the page ready for their order. "Food, dry goods, cloths? No spirits in my store. Only warning you in case you want whiskey, we're all good people around here. Prohibition days, you know."

Fred twisted his hands scanning the room for a trapdoor to a cellar. His eyes stopped at the woman at the other end of the counter.

"That's my wife, Margie. She thinks she's boss around here. Best behave around her as she's a fine woman." Margie's puckered lips looked suspicious of the strangers. She was a no-nonsense, full-figured woman who had an aura of sensibility. With a keen sense of people, she knew they were trouble by the big one's gestures.

"We're on the lookout to stake claim for a friend. I mean, we're interested in a treasure," Fred said.

"Have any lying around?" Tom piped in. "I see you have everything one could need on those shelves."

"Almost everything I suppose. No treasure though. If we had one ourselves, we would not be running a store. Lots of treasure hunters come through here. What will you be needing? Shovels, picks?" The door bells jingled as a perfumed breeze drifted in with the autumn air.

Margie strode joyfully across the floor to greet her client. "Welcome, Theresa, I was expecting to see you today. Congratulations on the birth of your niece. Did it all go well? Are mother Irene and daughter resting comfortably? Pearl? I heard she was named. All of you are so accomplished. Your brother, the historian, and his fine wife, who sings so beautifully in the choir, are finally making a little history of their own."

"You're a sight for sore eyes!" Tom whistled under his breath. The young lady looked so sweet and innocent as his nose twitched at the odd odor that drifted by. Something had shifted in his awareness. He wasn't feeling like his usual self.

"Allow me to show you this porcelain tea set, it just arrived from England." Margie ushered her to the alcove with a hand sweep. "This way Theresa, follow me. Your June wedding is around the corner. I can just hear the church bells ringing in the village square, with the flower gardens in full bloom. Oh, you must be so excited."

Theresa blushed with a demure smile.

"I heard your relatives from Toronto are coming by train. They run an antique store, is that right? Maybe they can give me a few tips on importing antiquities from overseas."

"I'm sure they'll be more than helpful."

Margie looked over her shoulder at the strangers. She reached around to loosen her laced corset under her dress by unsnapping one fastener discreetly. She knew all the right moves with constrictive attire. Margie placed the store's specialty order for all the fashion magazines.

The ladies caught up on the gossip. They stepped into an oval room, with its attractive window display for people passing by outside. Imported tea and sugar biscuits on a silver platter awaited them, surrounded by bright pink velvet chairs with fancy legs.

The shopkeeper focused on his customers. "So, you're treasure hunters seeking your fortune? There's thousands of islands that can have buried treasures along these shores. Or, even ancient artifacts and holy relics. Sacred treasures buried by the Templar's Knights that journeyed from across the Atlantic to hide them. We've all heard the fabled stories over the years. Blackbeard, Captain Kidd, Bluebeard, all the bearded pirates are said to have buried treasures here.

The ocean knows the secrets of many shipwrecks. Some of them were British ships with pay for the soldiers in the War of 1812. Lots of hidden coins and jewels on these shores and in these waters, my friends. A few islands are known to tweak the heart of a curious mind. Pieces of pottery, an arrowhead might be found, but not worth the sweat effort it takes to unearth them. Many have lost their lives in an endless pursuit of the mysteries of the past. They've come from all over the world. I've seen the disappointment in their eyes when they leave empty handed. Even broke. But some find ancient coins and sometimes even more."

Tom had a far-away look in his eyes—vague and eerily persistent—as he took in every word.

"The ships that have been wrecked along these shores often carried treasure. Spanish galleons, bringing gold and silver from the mines of Mexico, got wrecked here regularly. You want to search the headlands near the reefs. That's where to look for treasure for my money. Not that I have ever found any of that either.

You look like decent folk. So, I'll let you in on a secret. The old ocean has a mind of its own, and it protects the lost and buried riches and sacred relics. Its temperament is unpredictable, like a woman. You never know when its calmness will turn into a deadly fury. And the cliffs and rocky shores are dangerous even for brave men.

Heard of a fella once, when I was just a kid, an old sea captain. Middle of the last century it would have been, long before your time or mine. They said he hung around the wharf, walked on the beaches, all hours of the day, and night too. No one ever saw him dig or anything, but everyone said he was looking for a treasure, maybe one he had buried himself when he was young, and he couldn't recollect where. Or, maybe he was looking for a woman, who knows. Maybe he was lost or crazy. He up and vanished one day.... Maybe found his treasure and went back home with it. Who knows.

Pirate treasure is the famous stuff people come for, but there are other treasures. I tell you, coal is real treasure in Nova Scotia. That is where the real money is these days. It takes hard work, long hours, dedication and temperance. Now, that's the real road to riches. All the wealthy people in Nova Scotia made their money in coal or lumber as well as the railroads and fisheries. But I can assure you the only treasure under this roof, the only chest of gold, is the goods we sell and the goodwill of our customers—at least that I know of."

Fred was speechless and dumbfounded by the shopkeeper's verbose and meandering talk, but he wasn't giving up that easy after his cross-country escape. He waited for a timely segue into the conversation.

"I've heard a rumor of a treasure chest once. It was found on a coastal island, long before my time, and it vanished mysteriously overnight—before anyone could even open it. The Thompson children had found it on the beach. Those islanders were superstitious folk. They believed the lighthouse was haunted and that a spirit stole it. Everyone moved away and the wooden lighthouse was replaced with an automatic electric arc light. The old tower was left for a ghost on the lookout for his lost ship." The shopkeeper's voice sank to a stop.

Fred clenched onto the paper in his fist. He wasn't going to leave empty handed. "Are you sure there's not a forgotten box in the backroom by chance? Or, buried in your basement under a trapdoor?"

"No cellar either my friends. But maybe there are some precious gems down there in the earth and gold too. Why not? That's if you can dig deep enough. But you would have to go down halfway to China I reckon, and you don't look like miners. Fellows, this store has been in my family for half a century. And, this foundation is stone solid. I'd know if something was hidden beneath me." His shoe clicked down on the pine floor and his arms swept out wide. "We've got all your needs just look around. Some say, cure alls too, after that cursed Spanish flu reached our shores."

While Fred talked with the man, Tom started to wander through the aisles, amazed at all the items, with neatly stocked: liniments, syrups, and vaporizers. Vanity creams, perfumes, hair tonics, even whisker clippers were all displayed in cabinets along one wall. His eyes were drawn to the far end of the store.

Tom walked over to admire an oil painting on the wall beside a door. It was of a captain that looked lost at sea. A light beam pierced through a small ceiling window and onto the captain's face. Tom sensed a calling to move toward it, but became distracted as he looked over his shoulder, where he caught a glimpse of a porcelain statue. It was in a glass cabinet in the alcove.

Curiosity got the better of him as he went over to see it. Struggling to read the words on the plaque at its base, the shopkeeper became wary and walked over, startling Tom out of his trance. The statue was of the mariners' ancient moon goddess in Greek mythology named Brizo.

"Now, that statue is not for sale. It's part of my wife's private collection in her reading room—gifts from antique dealers passing through. But the painting you were eying is for sale. It came from a local estate." He put the pencil in his apron pocket and walked over. A foot ladder stood beneath the portrait. Steadying himself after the climb, he placed the heavy framed portrait onto a table as it leaned up against the wall.

"Its fairly good I reckon. I don't know much about art myself. But the frame's the real find here. Look at the hand-crafted detailing.... It's a one-of-a-kind, rare in a frame this size. You could take out the captain's painting, and use the frame for a grand portrait of yourself. It'll impress everyone who sees what a fine gentleman you are. It might even charm a lady or two."

Tom stared at the portrait before him. The oil painting was hypnotic with the captain's floodlit face. Tom's blue eyes glazed over with a vague memory of waking up on a sandy patch of a rocky beach as a statue swept up beside him. With choking breaths, he knew he was barely alive on an island called Oyster Secret.

Tom was pulled into his reverie. The captain's eyes started to dilate, widening to the frame's edge as it faded in-and-out. He took a step forward. Now nose-to-nose with the portrait, the pounding of his own heart was thunderous. A soft wind whistle was coaxing him to get on with it. The Invisibles were running out of time as the anticipated life ripples were intercepting at precise intervals bubbling throughout time and space.

The shopkeeper saw that Tom was in no hurry. He went to go polish some brass candlesticks on a nearby shelf. Most treasure hunters were not in a rush, and they came expecting to spend at least a few weeks on the hunt. Usually in summer though, not with the winds of winter blowing around their feet. They must be expecting to stay the season, or are not very bright.

Still in ear range, the shopkeeper shouted out, "You and your friend can rent a room from widow Sally during your stay. She runs the local Inn. Fresh sheets weekly and only a short walk to the outhouse. All the comforts of home. You may never want to leave. It's clean and tidy and Sally can sure cook up an east coast storm. You won't go hungry. Now that's a guarantee." Tom didn't hear the offer as Fred rushed down the aisle.

"Did you find it, boy?"

"Yes." Tom spoke in a dry whisper.

"I'm looking boy, that's no treasure, it just some seaman on a ship long gone I suppose. Mind you ... the frame might be worth something. Real gold? Hey, that captain looks a lot like you."

Tom couldn't resist the urge as his finger reached toward the portrait. Upon touching it, he heard the noise of a door opening as his body dematerialized. He was suctioned into a twirling vortex in a ripple's edge. The sound of a muted clap of thunder and a puff of smoke came from where the painted canvas was, and where Tom had vanished through. The shopkeeper looked up startled by the sound, then down at Fred passed out on the floor.

"Are you OK? What's going on?" The shopkeeper's face filled with horror as his jaw dropped and eyes scoped the room with suspicion. "Where did your friend go? Trying to charm my senses? I must ask you to leave. No funny magic tricks in my store. Now where is he?"

Fred stood up slowly as panic set in out of confusion. His brow wrinkled in fright. Aghast he trembled, with his white-knuckled hands gripping his head. The room had vanished for a second and Tom was gone.

Sam, the shopkeeper snapped his fingers under Fred's nose. He looked at the empty table. The portrait was gone. "Trying to trick me? Steal from me? Speak up!"

"I'm not sure what happened...." Fred's voice stuttered. Margie came running over to see what the commotion was about. She was beside herself, with her hands on hips almost breathless from huffing....

"We don't want no shenanigans in here! Get out of my store!" Sam added as his wife gave him the look. He grunted recalling magician Harry Houdini's Maritime tour years ago. "Monkey business, that's all it is."

Fred looked down every aisle, even the forbidden backroom as he uttered to himself, "I've lost it all right. There are places like that for me—heard they're worse than jail. I was warned it could happen at my age. Maybe I came into the store alone. And, Tom is outside. He said something about a carnival and took off. Is that it?" Sam was pumping a fist at him from down the aisle. Fred broke into a sweat as his heart raced him to the front door.

"I'm leaving.... Sorry I must be in the wrong place." Fred turned to look back and in his haste, bumped into widow Sally coming into the store. Fred knocked the elegant woman onto the floor, exposing her petticoats.

Fred's face was nervously shiny as his hand slapped his own cheek in disbelief. "I am so-so sorry ma'am!" Fred fumbled for words. He had not touched a woman in nearly four years. Their eyes met and his heart skipped a beat as her kind face made him feel warm and fuzzy inside. Fred's mouth watered from the aroma of bread. She was delivering the baked goods to Margie and Sam. He wiped the drool from the corner of his mouth.

"Did anything break?" Fred helped her up to her feet.

"I'm fine, honestly I am." Sally's voice was sweet. With a sweep of her arm, her dress puffed out above her ankles. She held a beaded purse in her hand.

"You have such innocent-looking eyes. Now, there's no need for such a solemn look, sir. It was an accident, wasn't it?"

Fred gave a silly bow and nod backing out the door with its familiar jingle. He stepped off the porch as his chin lifted up. Mabel the local librarian hurrying along, stopped to look up over Fred's shoulder. She covered her mouth in awe at the most extraordinary sight she had ever seen as her silver-rimmed glasses slipped down her nose. Mabel patted down her fluttering heart.

A magnificent double rainbow stretched over the Village of Chester. Brilliant, fiery colors splashed across the skies as it stretched far across the ocean. People poured into the streets to observe a lifetime miracle.

Sam stood on his front porch. Bewildered, a summer carnival poster caught his eye. He tore it off the post. Dumbfounded, he scratched his forehead. Margie's suspicious raised brow look was right all along. They were up to no good. But, how the other man and the portrait had vanished before him, he couldn't explain— let alone describe what he's seeing now.

Margie and Theresa watched from the bay window.

"Who was that gentleman?" Sally's hand fanned her face and neck excitedly, waiting for a reply...

"A lone stranger passing through that's all." Sam wanted to forget the incident for his own peace of mind.

"I'm looking for an honest and hardworking man to manage my Inn. I think he might be the one by his burly build." Sally's sly smile spoke a thousand words that Sam knew all too well. Her uncle ran the local jail. She had developed a fine sense of people from him.

❈

Fred retracted his steps past the fountain for a mile. The red automobile was gone and there were no tire tracks either. His heart raced with confusion as he spotted the local sheriff and his constables, waiting for him under the welcome to the Village of Chester sign. Fred knew he was in big trouble.

"Maybe I've lost it. My memory escapes me, I must have traveled here alone and there was no nephew named Tom, my sister Anna's son. The shopkeeper was trying to trick me. That's it! When I fell down in his store, I must've messed up my head. Phew! I knew it all along."

Fred's hefty frame lowered onto one knee in prayer pose. With a hard squint, he faced the ocean glare to make a wish on the rainbow. He heard about this as a child during story time, but never tried it before. I have no treasure, so nothing to lose, ran through his mind.

"If there's a goddess around help me.... OK? I only need a fresh start. That's all. I'm an innocent man most of the time. It'll make my mother proud of me, wherever she is. How about this one tiny favor?"

Zephyr heard the faint cry for his eternal love. With a mighty blow, the Invisible whistled across the water's surface as a tiny ripple made his wish come true. Clouds rolled in over the deity's shadowy presence casted upon the land as it whooshed across the horizon.

As the authorities stepped toward him. Fred's legs buckled and his eyes rolled back. He fell to the ground motionless as his head barely missed a jagged rock. The constables shook their heads at his luck as he came to. Fred opened his eyes not knowing what had happened. He felt somewhat different and hungry. They lifted him up by his elbows and put him in their paddy wagon.

Sally heard the news from her uncle. The next day she came by the jailhouse with a hot meal for him and posted his bail. She knew that there was something special about this man. He was only a little confused. Fred bumped his head passing out near the village's welcome sign. He was left with no memory of who he was or where he came from, or a person named Tom in an automobile. But, he knew his name was Fred and that he was an honest and hardworking man. And, that was good enough for Sally.

It wasn't long before the judge dismissed the case against Fred. There were no witnesses to tie him to the stolen portrait.

Fred was happy but confused by the accusation.

Fred had room and board at Sally's Inn in exchange for work. He was a handyman and a good fixer on the property. The locals hired him to do minor repair work. Sally's friends knew that he won her heart.

Soon after he moved in, they fell in love over breakfast. With a mouthful of warm buttered bread and a dollop of berry jam, he took her hand in his. They were married in the village square the following summer.

The Inn, three doors down from Sam's general store, was the original location of his store about two decades earlier. The store had moved into Sam's father's rambling house, after his father died. Margie oversaw the renovations with a keen eye. With the extra space, they expanded their selection of imported tableware, crystal and fashion collections.

Sally had asked Fred to replace a rotting wallboard. Steep steps led him into the basement. The root cellar in the far corner was fully stocked for the winter months. With a lit candlestick holder, Fred looked around bent low under the ceiling. It was easy enough to find as he pulled hard exposing a dugout that contained a latched wooden box full of trinkets. At first he thought it was a treasure. But it was mostly junk of sentimental things to someone with no real value.

Fred traded it with Sam for some supplies, with Margie's approval. He in turn sold some to locals and to passing tourists. One old-looking amulet, along with several pieces of furniture from the basement of the old rambling house was sold to Gora's son. He had inherited the antique store in Toronto. He would come to the eastern shores every two years on a purchasing trip.

Sally and Fred passed away within days of each other during a flu outbreak one winter at the close of the second world war. They had married too late for children, and with Fred having never regained any memories from before coming to Chester, their estate passed to Sally's closest relative: a sister who had married into the Gora family. The contents of the Chester Inn were sorted, and items that could sell for a fair price in Toronto's antique market were shipped by the railway, while the rest was sold or donated locally.

They were buried in a small cemetery above a cliff overlooking the ocean. In the distance across the bay, a lighthouse on an island kept vigil.

There is only so much energy in the universe as it moves around, changes form, and is constantly recycled. The same energy manifests itself in different ways at different times, but it is always the same energy.

Just as each rainbow is unique in a different place and in a different sky, it always has the same colors in the same order. So too does each sevenfold manifestation of a given life energy that shares similarities if we can perceive them.

In this world, the energy is constrained. It cannot be in two places at the same time and must find ways of moving from one locus—point or curve—to another one. Sometimes it can do so smoothly and quietly, and sometimes there is a thunderclap and the world skips a beat.

Zephyr had trapped young Tom's energy in the portrait with the captain's, and used the combined energy to spirit the painting to another place, where Zephyr and Bastet could continue to keep an eye on the progress of my story.

- CHAPTER 12 -

Toronto, spring 2022

It was late afternoon, only a few days after Margie's opening gala. I had missed out on the celebration. Tom raved about the antique displays, and the eclectic guests with their stories of buying trips abroad. It brought him into fits of laughter as he repeated the escapades to me. Tom brought over a taste of the party: a platter of mouth-watering savory and sweet canapés. Margie sure knows how to throw a memorable bash.

Tom was psyched up as my finger dabbed up the last few pastry crumbs on the platter. He burst into an animated stance and offered to walk the cat for me. Somewhat surprised I took him up on it. This gave me the chance to take advantage of my virtual-streaming membership of world-famous museum exhibits.

Probably a domesticated stray, but with the prowling instinct of a feral cat, Baster needed an occasional afternoon excursion. I told Tom not to veer from the route I had given him as this feline had her routine.

After they left, I looked out the window. She was exhibiting unusual moves of prowess with each step, and her particularly long neck and upright tail took on an air of confidence from this viewpoint.

A suburbanite at heart, Tom found it comical to walk a cat, but City Bylaw doesn't allow for animals off-leash in this district. By her strut it was obvious Baster enjoyed going past the city parks and the bustling outdoor cafés, with its enticing smells. She had an aloof charm about her and people would admire her with a smile or a nod, but heaven help anyone who tried to pat her. I had warned Tom. He knew to discourage outreaching hands.

As I powered down my laptop, I caught a glimpse of them outside. What perfect timing, I marveled, watching Tom step up onto the porch. I couldn't hear him but he looked strange crouched so low, with a stern-looking finger pointed at her nose.

"I know you understand every word I say. Look cat, next time, no snarls at strangers, or I'll tell Irene all about it. I can't do much if you pick a fight with another leashed animal, but the police and the veterinarian can." Baster plunked herself down beside him on the steps. "Let's make a truce. Agreed? Behave yourself next time—let's be friends—I'm around for a while."

"Back so soon?" I called out through the open window as the sun began its descent.

"That was some experience, I'll be right up. I've made reservations at the jazz club for seven, there's an amazing trio playing tonight." Tom hoped she didn't overhear him reprimanding her cat, and as if a cat understood him. Tom fumbled with the key to the building's entryway. Baster took advantage of his distraction. She walked in circles to tangle the leash around his legs. Tom lost his balance and tripped down the few steps.

Tom found himself flat on the ground as Baster slipped slyly out of her collar. Tom's arm was wrapped up in his jacket. When he tried to unzip it to disentangle himself, the zipper caught on the chain that hung out of his inside pocket. It glittered bright then it was gone— and so was Baster.

"No! Wait, Baster!" But it was too late. She had sprung up, with the amulet dangling from her mouth. Tom struggled to get up and in doing so, his glasses slipped off his nose. He could not find them in the evening shadows. By now he lost sight of the cat, but the sound of a chain being dragged on the asphalt set him into motion. He jumped up onto his feet.

Baster leaped over a garbage dumpster only to vanish around the corner. Tom caught a glimpse of her and was in pursuit, without his glasses. She led Tom on a merry chase through the side streets down toward the waterfront. The damp ground was slick with mud and dead leaves under darkening skies.

I leaned out the window in dismay. I couldn't believe what I was seeing. It was time for action as the tensor bandage tightened around my ankle. I gave it a final pull and tucked it in. With my sneakers on, I took a shortcut through the building's back door.

"Tom, where are you?" I walked briskly down the road. My hips tottered as my arms propelled me onward, surprised that my leg didn't go into spasm. With the alley in front of me, I turned left at the crossroad as my mind raced ahead of me ... straight down the street toward the construction site close to Khilto's. Had Baster led Tom back to where I had found her?

Distracted from my thoughts, my eyes darted around to track down a creaking noise as squealing rats scurried into an open wall vent of an Art Deco feather factory, that was being gutted for expensive lofts. My hand covered my nose from the stench of the toppled garbage cans. Broken bricks piled up beside a fire escape ladder, caught my eye on my way over to the quarry.

A perfumed breeze whirled around me as a shadowy figure appeared in a mist. Its presence splintered forming into millions of images. I watched splendid and shocking events from prehistoric to modern time—and far into the future. I couldn't keep up with all that I was seeing. Is this a life review? In that moment, I recalled a childhood story about invisible deities with fragrance-laced wings. The experience dispelled as Tom rushed toward me saying, "Irene, are you OK?"

Although I had come looking for him, Tom's presence startled me. Baster jumped out of his arms as she caught sight of me. Tom tried to comfort me in his embrace but I stiffened. Something was stirring inside his jacket that made me uneasy. The way he kissed me was a telltale sign that something had frightened him.

We walked up to my building, with Baster in my arms, her collar and leash were on the front porch. There was a grinding crunch as I stepped toward it. Tom wore a vacant, defeated expression at the sound. I felt his heart drop as his mind raced from whatever had shocked him, to the problem of his broken glasses underfoot. They were crucial for his early morning meeting. Baster slipped out of her collar, was all that he could say.

"Oh, Tom!" I picked up the frames and a glass shard.

"It's not your fault."

"I'm sorry."

Tom was transfixed by the cat's stare as I opened the entryway door with an uneasy silence. We made our way up the three flights of stairs. Tom walked behind me as he wrestled with his common sense. He felt the amulet in his inside pocket and let his mind wander: *If I told Irene what had happened, she would think I'm crazy. And, even more crazy to have a good luck charm. I'm upset enough about the ordeal. I have to stop second-guessing myself. This is not an ordinary cat, and Irene must already know it.*

Tom's muddy shoes landed on the rubber mat as I slid the chain lock into place. He called the club to cancel our reservations. We weren't in the mood to go out. The entire episode had taken less than an hour, but it feels never-ending as if it was only the beginning....

Tom walked down the hall to the washroom without a word. Baster broke the tension with her speedy circuits, skidding around the furniture. She was hungry and this was her signal to be fed. I replenished her bowls in the kitchen for the night. I heard the toilet flush and running water followed by his getting-ready-for-bed noises in the bedroom. The box frame finally squeaked then silenced as he plunked down.

I knew it was going to be an unsettling night and Tom didn't prove me wrong. He was awake most of it with the blinds half-opened as usual. Shadows shuffled on the ceiling, into the early hours. When he did catch a few winks, he had incoherent and disturbing flashbacks of the cat's glowing eyes on a statuesque figure as she spoke with him of an ancient goddess in a murky tunnel.

Tom's eyes opened with a start. He leaped out of bed after what felt like only a few minutes of rest. It was an overcast morning and a big day for him. Although semi-awake, I was startled as his feet thudded onto the floor. Last night felt unreal with Baster's escape, and with my momentary vision, or was it an imaginary night terror, that had made me wonder if an Invisible had tried to contact me. But, I was glad that it was daybreak, and that Baster was asleep on my side of the bed.

"Today's the day!" Tom shouted out over the loud blast from the wall-mount shower spout. The water trickled down the checkered tile stall as the steam was sucked into a ceiling vent. I put a towel around his neck as he stepped out pulling him in close for a kiss before we switched places. I cupped his chin lovingly then dragged the shower curtain across the circular rod.

The towel was wrapped around his waist. Tom combed his hair with a dab of hair gel. He continued to rehash the experience, spitting toothpaste into the sink. Nothing made sense of last night no matter how he looked at it. Tom walked into the bedroom to get dressed. By now he had a designated corner of the closet, a dresser drawer, and a spot for his toothbrush in the bathroom.

It was only a reflection from the spotlight above the chain-link fence along with my not having my glasses. Or was Baster a shape-shifter? That's ridiculous even to imagine. What's come over me? Maybe I've been watching too much apocalyptic and post-apocalyptic fiction content the last few years. With his questionable mind-chatter, Tom zipped up his pants almost convinced by his rational mind.

Tom called out from the bedroom. "Work today?"

"Yes, it's flower shop day." I raised my voice over the hairdryer with my head upside-down. I flipped my hair over and brushed it out. With the cord rolled up, I hung the dryer on the wall hook. I walked into the bedroom.

Dressed and ready to face the day, I stood in front of the hall mirror in red flats, black denim pants and a paisley blouse. I wish I knew what had happened at the construction site. Whatever it was, it wasn't good.

Tom still wore a shell-shocked look that reminded me of the veterinarian's expression at the animal clinic, after Baster's last and only check-up last year. I never knew what had happened in the examining room either. I had only stepped out of the room for a moment. I watched Tom in the mirror approach me from behind. To be playful, I swung around and fussed with his tie.

"I'll drop by the optician close to my office. The sign in their window says they offer an hour guarantee on new frames. They'll even give you a beverage and a donut while you wait. Now, that's service."

"Do they open early?"

"Seven o'clock."

"Your meeting will start on schedule!"

"That's good news and time to spare." Tom's phone beeped with a text message. He scrolled down somewhat surprised as I walked into the kitchen. "It's a message from Fred!" Tom hollered from across the room. "Sally has called it quits time-out again. He said it wasn't pleasant, but I've heard this all before. After the theater, she made a big scene at a restaurant."

"Sally's totally smitten with him, I don't get it. She couldn't say enough good things about him. I'm sure they'll work it out, they always do." I turned off the kitchen faucet as it squeaked shut. I walked to the front door with a glass of water and a bottle of pills for Tom. It was obvious by his expression, he needed one. He opened the bottle and shook out a pill.

Baster poked her head around the corner to watch. Tom began to feel uneasy again in the front foyer. He felt for the amulet in his jacket pocket to make sure the cat hadn't stolen it again. Yesterday was a nightmare that still haunted him.

With the pulsating aura of an oncoming migraine, he had managed to get his act together in a sporty suit. This was a once-in-a-lifetime meeting with his most important client and investors. Tom had to be at the top of his game to salvage his business.

A minute before seven Tom's phone dinged. A text flashed that his ride was downstairs, waiting under dreary skies. In a slight cough, he admitted the water washed down the bitter taste of the painkiller. Tom was in such a hurry that he almost tripped over the umbrella stand.

He swung his laptop bag over his shoulder and gave me his usual salute. I thought more about my experience last night as I chain-locked the door behind him. I slid down to the floor with arms wrapped around my knees and wondered.

Baster watched me from the sofa.

I would take the bus to work later.

~~~~

Bastet my friend, and Zephyr my eternal companion, I felt your presence skim along the ripples of this realm, and I also sensed other Invisibles from our sanctuary watch with anticipation of the enfolding and unfolding of human ripples in this space-time continuum.

In 1868 when the Khilto ran aground in downtown Toronto. You planned it well Zephyr. You made sure the statue I had entrusted to the St. Lawrence River would arrive safely, and be hidden away until the time was right. And today, Bastet, you brought it, and me with it, back into the sunshine.

The ripples on the pond spread and weaken, but there is only one pond and when the ripples intersect, they can form a powerful node. Like a sunbeam on the water, I skip backward and forward, from wave crest to wave crest, reflecting and refracting rainbows as I go.

But as all luminous colors balance out its ratios in the end to form a beam of silver light, all eventually slip into the darkness and transform awaiting a spiraling return in the future or in the past.

~~~~~~

- CHAPTER 13 -

Toronto, autumn 1925

The letter was addressed to Mrs. Pearl Irene Karmen. It had been more than fifty years since my father died, that I had only seen my middle name Irene on legal documents. He used to call me Irene when he was upset with me. It was the final eviction notice. I have been counting the days on my calendar. It was if it was only yesterday when I arrived in Toronto, with one suitcase, a dome-top trunk, and a broken heart.

I had already scoured through the upper two floors of the house. The brick and stone basement with its retired coal and oil-fired furnaces, was never used for storage. The moment had come to tackle the attic with cherished memories. There could be nothing there worth selling, but there might be a memento or two with sentimental value. Although I could not take much with me to the rooming house, I would regret not checking.

I climbed the stairwell to the attic as my knees endured the challenge. I hung onto the railing for dear life. Thank goodness there's a small landing halfway up between floors to catch my breath. I had not remembered the stairs as so narrow and steep, so frightening.

When I was young, in the days after father died, my next-door neighbor Mabel and I would climb up to this place with her six-year-old daughter Sally for story time. Together, all three of us would squeeze into a huge cushioned armchair with Sally's stuffed animal, a rabbit she called Brizo. Sally had named her after a fabled story of an ancient lunar goddess who was a protector of seafarers of the seven seas, and worshiped by the women of the Greek Island of Delos during the Age of Gemini.

We read her stories from lavishly illustrated books of the Arabian Nights and Treasure Island, and Mabel would tell us the most enchanting stories that she made up in her own head. She would stir in elements of these stories, together with her wild fancies, and the news of the day that she heard from the newspaper boys, hawking their broadsheets on the street corner.

But time passed and Sally grew up. She felt she was too big for fairy tales and old women. I was in my late thirties. They eventually moved away when Mabel's husband's employer transferred him to the company's head office in Montreal. We lost touch over the years.

I thought of Sally and a blue cloth-covered book. That glimpse of her from my deep subconscious inspired me. There wasn't much time left under this roof. I must see that book again. It was surely in the attic for I would never have thrown it out. When I reached the top of the stairwell and heaved the door open on its rusty hinges, I found the light bulb had burned out.

Flicking the wall switch furiously as if that could somehow repair the delicate tungsten filament, I remembered there's a flashlight in the kitchen. A workman had left it long ago. I climbed back down the stairs again. And, I rummaged around in the kitchen drawers.

Found it!

Back at the top of the stairwell, I stepped into .... Well, certainly no Aladdin's Cave, though it bore a jumbled resemblance. There were decades-old boxes stacked along the narrow sloping space between the eaves, and mirrors, lamps, fur coats and sequined dresses spilling out of chests. Shelves held books, dominoes and checkers games and my Ouija board. Frilly gowns from parties long forgotten, were draped over a wood-folding card table.

But the mirrors were cracked, the lamps in need of re-wiring, and the furs and dresses exuded the pungent presence of mothballs. I passed a rusted, chipped enameled sink. I had a vague recollection of when it was ripped out of the kitchen in favor of a modern stainless-steel sink. Then, a scratching sound of feet startled me. A squirrel's eyes glowed briefly in the floodlight beam, from my flashlight, before the curious spectacle scurried out of sight through a hole in the board wall.

I noticed Casper's wooden cigar box. I hesitated to open the memento, but I did. Soon, I placed it down beside his other things on the floor. I could never open those fanciful valentine cards inside nor discard them.

At the end of the main room, I turned a crystal doorknob to enter the inner sanctum. Memories flooded in as I envisioned my younger life in this house.

I switched off the flashlight. The afternoon sun cast a warm glow in the small uncluttered room. Faint dust particles danced in a shaft of light as I looked around eagerly for any telltale signs of childhood. Father had set it up as his secret hideaway, where he could read in private. After he died, I felt his comforting presence in this room. It became my sanctuary that I shared with Mabel and Sally. Father's leather top desk was in one corner and an armchair in the other. Books were stacked on Edwardian pedestal table beside it. My fingers strummed along the spines to a blue cloth-covered book.

That's it!

Leaves of a Portrait. The title reminded me of Queen Victoria's famous *Leaves From a Journal*, in which she had published notes from her diaries of her life in Balmoral in the Scottish Highlands. I had read it avidly as had many of her loyal subjects in those days. Perhaps hers had inspired this book's title?

I removed the sheet covering the armchair and plunked myself down. This was a magical place for dreams to come true. Whoever can finish the book will know the treasure's secret, was what Mabel had told Sally. And that's exactly what I need to distract me from my woes. A good story.

The afternoon sun was comforting as I picked up Brizo from a footstool, removing her from under a sheeted hiding place. I squeezed the plush toy to awaken the goddess. Sally's friend had been alone in this room for decades, but never forgotten.

The book's title was the same, but it seemed somehow changed, different. Funny how aging memories are molded by time until the original is barely recognizable? But then I had never read this book myself. Father read it to me when I was little, and Mabel read it to Sally and me. But, I had never held it myself before this day.

I wondered why? I snuggled into the cushioned seat, Brizo beside me. Daylight flooded the room. The hand-stitched spine cloaked the book's mystique as I opened it. My silver-rimmed spectacles slid down my nose. I saw that it was handwritten with a quill and ink. I realized it was actually someone's journal. But why did father have it and read it to me? And why did Mabel read it to Sally?

Now, that was a mystery in itself.

Oh, there on the next page, the memoirist identified himself: Captain Pearl of Oyster Secret. I remember some of his story. The linen paper was soft, heavy and rich in my fingers, but yellowed with age. Its musty aroma spoke of its decades in this attic. My heart fluttered with the innocent feeling of childhood. To dream from a child's mind consoled me. I was worried about my future although there weren't many years left for me.

Why I waited all these years to return to this room is not a mystery. Life got busy and then I forgot. Perhaps I had grown out of my fantasy, and no longer needed the comfort of father's presence. But now as the end of my time in this house approached, I needed to feel it once again, one last time in this place.

Nervous energy ran through me as my fingers tingled with curiosity. It was a memoir after all. True stories of someone's life. I turned the page and began the story that took place long ago. Page by page, I read it throughout the afternoon as the sun sank below the houses on the opposite side of the street. I was absorbed in his words that plunged deep into human emotion.

I paused to pat the book with uncertainty to the rattle of the window frame. A red-tailed hawk had landed on the ledge. I imagined the breeze the bird's wingspan had caused as the feathers folded neatly into its sleek frame. There was something mysterious about its intelligent eyes that peaked my interest. It was strange behavior for a raptor to spy on a human. But with Brizo tucked in beside me brought childhood comfort.

How appropriate she's with me. Right captain? This was your journal, or perhaps it's more of a memoir. I see its not in the form of a daily diary, but rather undated narrative entries spanning over many years like little stories.

And it also was my mother's. She had used the blank pages at the end to write her own story. And, I had never read it before. When father read it to me, he never read the last several pages, the ones mother had written in with her flowing script, so unlike the captain's bold masculine pen.

Some of the captain's stories were vaguely familiar though reading it myself, I realized father had always embellished it, skipping some slower parts, and adding richness and detail to others of more interest to a little girl. So had Mabel, reading it to Sally.

From what I can gather, the captain started composing his memoir shortly after he had returned to London. The captain was an educated man. He wrote captivating, descriptive vignettes about other adventures from his youth. It was long before his ship called the Khilto, was wrecked in a freak storm in the South Pacific in the year 1820. He had been sailing to an island only he knew, where the natives dove for the best pearls in the world.

He had named the island Oyster Secret, and the fame and fortune his pearls bought him in the markets of the Netherlands and Barcelona is how he came to be known as Captain Pearl.

I was only twenty when my beloved Tom had also set sail on a ship called Khilto. Now, that's quite a coincidence, two vessels with the same name. Hmm, it seems that the next entries, with some water stains, are about his life after his fated shipwreck.

Entry....

By a crackling fire in my London home, here I sit at my writing desk. I no longer find comfort from my possessions.

My nightly headaches have not ceased with a recurring dream. Memories of that torrential downpour is a never-ending nightmare I no longer can escape. I do not recall washing up on shore, but I remember the blinding light when my eyes opened to a luminous halo beside me.

It's as if it was only yesterday, when I lay under a fiery, summer rainbow and felt the presence of a spirit force that had saved me. The islanders on Oyster Secret helped me regain my health. A fragmented memory of my crew still haunts me. It was mutiny. There is no resolve in my heart....

Entry....

There was one beautiful island girl named Alene. I had lived some time on the island, falling in love then losing my girl to prowling pirates. Her newborn was left motherless, when the islanders took the child into their care.

I cherish this one memory of holding Alene in my arms. I had told her in secrecy that my given name was Thomas. It's an ancient Aramaic word meaning twin; a look alike.

Once we sat by the firepit where I spoke of a family myth that I had once heard. It was passed down from my great grandfather as it had been told to him. This name, Thomas, was given to planet Earth from the star beings in the constellation Gemini, during the Age of Gemini that ruled over the Medieval Times for 2000 years, from 6000 BC on.

~~~~~

I was named after my grandfather, as this given name must skip a generation. After I completed my formal education, I followed in his footsteps, and became a sea captain. Those given this first name of mine were undying conquerors that sought after adventure. Alene believed in the moon and the stars as guiding lights and invisible protectors of fate. Her eyes twinkled bright with my words.

But to everyone else I told her, I was known as Captain Pearl. A descendant of a powerful family that made their fortune from international business and trade on land and at sea, with their own fleet of ships. I commissioned the most majestic ship to be built. The name Khilto was a word I had heard in a dream at a young age.

Entry....

I'd observe the ship's figurehead each day for its peculiar behavior. It was of a mariners' goddess. But it changed form as if possessed by a spirit. Perhaps from the crews' prayers for a safe passage. The goddess must have saved me, but why I could not answer.

Instinct drove me to take the statue with me on the next passing vessel. I packed it carefully in a carved wooden chest that Alene had made under the stars, only days before she was taken. Enchanted with good fortune I hoped, it became a sort of good luck talisman.

~~~~~

Entry....

My youth was slipping away after I left Oyster Secret. I sailed the seas in search of Alene, and eventually ran aground in London, where I settled for a time. Still, empty inside. I made a small fortune working with friends of my father, in the Society of Lloyd's maritime insurance business.

The lifestyle of a businessman and a gambler took its toll. I frequented the gentleman's club, burlesque and vaudeville establishments until I became a recluse. In 1835 my employ ended. My portrait was commissioned as a retirement present. I took it as a sign and an omen. A farewell gift. I set sail as a first class passenger on a merchant ship destined to the New World. I had heard Alene may be in Nova Scotia.

Entry....

I am sailing on a long voyage, never to return without my Alene, my pearl. I am writing in my journal from my private cabin crossing the Atlantic. I sold my London house and all its contents not long ago, taking with me only a purse of silver and gold coin, a few furnishings, a chest of clothes and other necessities. I secured down the figurehead's chest. The waves are fierce and angry tonight, with its pounding thrashes against my porthole. It makes for another restless sleep. Challenged to steady my quill pen, I must end here, kisses to you my love...

~~~~~~

Entry....

The ship docked at the Halifax port. The pungent smell of fish and smoke burned my eyes. I looked up and down the wharf at ships loading and unloading their cargo in an orderly manner. A skinny boy stood before me. He was eager for my attention, pulling on my top coat. He took his cap off with a bow. He knew of a suitable rooming house for me.

So, for a half-copper penny, the boy grabbed the leather handles of my possessions one at a time, and lugged them onto his cart. I followed him down the road. It was his widow mother's rooming house and he was a good working boy. She was a good cook with three children. It was close to the general store. Time to rest and hold you in my dreams.

Entry....

So, I end this journal within these walls, with my portrait before me. I had searched the coast endlessly, but cannot find you, Alene. When I look into my eyes of the painting, I see the yearning for your kiss. My heart spills out these words, before I blow out this candle. The inkwell is empty and no pennies left to fill it. I will be leaving here at sunrise.

My mother taught me to believe in fate. I will not fail you my love. If I must, I'll wait for you in the heavens. You'll always be the pearl of my heart, my dearest Alene. Sweet dreams, farewell....

~~~~~

I was pulled further into his unfolding past. I realized that the captain's last few entries had been composed, not in just any rooming house, but in the very rooming house my mother, Peggy, had grown up in. And, this explained how this journal came to be here, and mother must have found it, or been given it.

Somehow, I could not bring myself to read her story right away. I sat for a time simply contemplating her clean, flowing writing, remembering her forcing my siblings and me to practice our writing, every day. I thought of what it must have been for her to grow up in a rooming house, rubbing elbows with rough men and fallen women.

Mother had aspired to a better life and fell in love and become married to a man she thought was a good catch for his fine education. Only in the last few years of her life did she know happiness and comfort in Toronto. Albeit only for a short time. She never knew the greater prosperity her husband, my father, would eventually enjoy in this house on Jarvis Street.

As I reflected back to my childhood my fingers felt the edge of an envelope hidden in a slit in the fabric of the back cover. There was a resistance to pulling it out, but I was also intrigued at the thought of who touched it last and what it could be.

I slipped it out and turned it over. It had never been opened. It had yellowed over the years and a corner was burnt. Was it tossed into a fireplace then retrieved quickly? Maybe second thoughts about its contents, but the writer felt a need to hide it in this room.

Maybe it's a message for me.

It's small and innocent enough but the notion of opening it now unnerved me. It was none of my business or was it? I'm not sure why as whoever wrote it must be long gone. Simply words on paper with no possible embarrassment for anyone still living. Still, I felt uneasy and I couldn't understand why. And why I felt compelled to read this memoir.

I let my fancy wander, imagining in turn if it was from my father writing to a lover, or perhaps a note from a housekeeper, a disgruntled tenant, or perhaps a squatter hiding from the law under my roof. I no longer have live-in staff or dogs to alert me of a stranger on the premises. I flipped the envelope over again, but nothing was written on either side.

I held it up toward my friend the hawk on the other side of the windowpane. The incoming light gave it enough transparency to see that the ink marks had bled through the folded paper. But I couldn't make out any words as Captain Pearl crossed my mind. Ever since I came home from the park yesterday, I haven't felt quite right. The air had a different feel. A certain quality to it as it rustled through the treetops.

I settled myself back into the chair and turned to the last five pages of the book. The ones with mother's writing.

~~~~~

She wrote....

When I was a child growing up in Halifax, my father was a sailor. He lost his arm when the ship he sailed on sank in a storm. He washed up on a South Pacific shore with bruises and cuts. The waves had dragged him over the coral reefs.

The ship's captain had not fared as well as his broken body lay on the beach. After kicking him a few times to vent their frustration, the crew left him for the corpse they thought he was. My father was not proud of that. He felt the captain deserved a decent burial, as the storm that had wrecked them was not his fault. But, the men were angry at their plight and took it out on his lifeless body.

My father and his crew mates found pearls and shells on the beach that they could use to buy passage back to Europe, or to the New World. One of father's companions found an amulet buried deep in the sand under the roots of a sprawling tree. They could not tell where it was from, or what it was made of, brass metal perhaps and stone. The glyphs around it seemed Egyptian or Chinese, not that any of the men could read English, let alone either of those languages.

The cuts on his arm festered. It was amputated to keep him alive. With no arm, he could no longer do the duty of a sailor, so he made his way to the New World, where a man with one good arm could make a living from the free land.

In Halifax, he did not find free land, but he did find a good woman, and settled down with her. Her father was not a wealthy man, as few were even in this land of opportunity. But, he did gift them a house for her dowry. And so, my mother met and married Abner.

In time, children came: Alfred, Peggy—that's me—and Robert. And in time, Abner suffered more and more from his arm, and was unable to keep even the meanest of employment. Distraught and in constant pain, he died one night in a brawl on the wharf.

Mother was left with us three young children, and only a house to get by with. So, she rented out rooms, changed the sheets, and made the meals. Some came for a night, some months. Mostly sailors, blowing on shore to sit out the worst of winter weather, or to take a short rest and woo some girl before heading back out to sea. Many were drunks, as many sailors are on shore, and some were rough, but all paid their copper pennies up front, or got no room.

But one was different. He was a sailor, true, but different from the others. There was a mist about his blue eyes, and a restlessness in his soul. Captain Pearl he called himself, and there were surely not two of that name. I never knew his given name. Still somewhat handsome with his aging face, he stood out as a somebody amongst the master tradesmen and journeymen that landed on the docks.

~~~~~~

After breakfast, Captain Pearl was out of the house during the day if the sun was shining. But on stormy days, he stayed in by the fire in the backroom, and would tell us children stories of pirates and treasure. He said that was what he was here for, to search for a lost treasure. Though mother claimed his eyes told a different story. A story of a lost love rather than of hidden gold.

One afternoon he told my mother that he had been robbed on the docks of his purse, which was possible enough in those days. He had a head wound to show for it. Halifax being a raw new city, mother allowed him to trade some of his possessions for room and board. He soon fell sick and was never the same.

Mother had me cleaning the rooms. That is how I came to see the captain's portrait in his room. Younger than when I knew him, but still with misty blue eyes, standing on the deck of his ship in a storm. I saw his chest of clothes, and a table of fine polished wood from England. There was a beautifully carved wooden box, perhaps three feet long bound in chains. It was his treasure chest.

It wasn't long before Captain Pearl had sold almost everything. Penniless, he left the house. He left a few things behind, and this journal was one of them. I sometimes saw him in a shabby coat on the street, or sleeping under the wharf. I heard later that spring that he had died. I always wondered what had happened to his portrait, and to his treasure chest. Sold for food and rent money, I assumed.

That spring and all of seventeen, I met and fell head over heels in love with Charles Thompson. He was five years my senior, and an educated young man who completed all his schooling right through grade school. Charlie had a bright future.

Soon married, and soon expecting our first child, we needed a place to live right away, so we became lighthouse keepers. It was to be for one year only, until Charlie's father could set him up in business. But his father soon died of pneumonia, and the business never happened. He had inherited a few things, enough to keep us going, and the one year in the lighthouse was soon twenty.

In the meantime, I had three children of my own: Fred, Pearl Irene, and Anna. And as I worked a patch of garden, and kept up our cabin and the lighthouse, Charlie worked for a few local businesses, keeping their books. But this was not the life he had imagined for himself.

Charlie had started to gamble and to lose. One night he gambled away our savings of forty dollars. It was around that time, the children dragged home a box wrapped in chains that they had found down on the beach.

I knew it at once as Captain Pearl's.

The captain's journal ended soon after he arrived in Halifax, with his purse stolen and him left destitute.

He must have sold his fine portrait of himself in exchange for a few nights of room and board. As a person of no fame in the New World, the frame was worth more than his likeness, but in the end, Captain Pearl, died a broken and lonely man, but not defeated as I suspect that he believed in fate like I do.

Was he the last named Thomas, of his family legacy?

My mother's pages ended here to.... She had run out of space.

Perhaps it continued in the letter?

- CHAPTER 14 -

Toronto, autumn 1925

By this time, darkness had fallen, and my friend the hawk had long since flown away. Pocketing the letter from the back of the journal, the flashlight's beam escorted me down the long circular descent. My foot touched down on the ceramic tile floor, with its dizzying pattern.

My gurgling stomach knew to keep me on schedule. With one foot in the kitchen, I closed the pantry door behind me. Water poured out smoothly from the steel faucet. Its warmth soothed my fingers over the sink beneath the window. I gazed out through the floral sheer curtain as I dried my hands on a tea towel.

Night was settling on the city, moonlight casting shadows in my overgrown backyard. I'll miss my cherry and magnolia trees' magnificent blooms next spring. This place brought me so much happiness, with the celebrations and joyous laughter. I composed myself, attempting to dismiss the nostalgia that kindled inside me. The yellowed curtain fluttered from my long sigh.

The bread loaf was in the breadbox, with spongy lemon biscuits that the bakery had delivered earlier on. Yellow cheese and slices of tomato, herbs from my garden, and a pinch of salt made the perfect sandwich, with a cup of tea to wash it down.

The kettle whistled its song.

It began as a restless night. I fantasized about a never-ending romance, and the sealed envelope. I dreamed that my Tom had sent me a message from the other side. I had fallen into a deep sleep cocooned in my flannel blankets and feather pillows. I awoke refreshed with the sunrise, and the melodious songs of the autumn birds.

I took it all in, listening to the branches brush gently across the window of my room. The workmen on the streetcar tracks down the street were on schedule. The hammering startled me up out of bed. My covers flung over to the side. I sat up with my legs dangling down.

The washroom down the narrow hall was my first morning stop. The floor squeaked its familiar tune. I walked past a richly gilded mirror that father had acquired from a store dealing in French furnishings.

Barefoot, my toes curled under to stop me. I was overcome with fright as my breath became labored. Was I alone in the house? The mirror was now behind me. It faced an empty wall.

I had a glimpse of a woman's reflection. Her angelic face so clear in my mind. My heels inched backward, retracing the few steps I had taken. Then, without hesitation, I turned to face my fear.

Almond-shaped eyes shimmered closer into the frame, with a finger to her lips ... her features, so striking. I too, was drawn in, to slip through the glass and listen to her whispers. A finger curled beaconing me. A premonition? A forewarning? Her lips moved but the words were inaudible. The lyrical tone was familiar, but ever so distant.... It was drifting in from far away. I shook myself out of the ridiculousness of it all.

But as soon as I thought that I must be seeing things, a luminous cloud fell upon her and the figure dilated into transparency. Panic set in. I was worried about my eyesight and being alone. And maybe insane?

Or, I must be having a stroke and sprawled out unconscious in my home. My eyes darted up and down the hallway. At least I wasn't lying flat out looking down at myself from the treetops. With my hands cupped over my eyes, I peered between my fingers with a sigh of relief.

I had confronted my own reflection in a worn nightgown and housecoat. It's only me. I must have caught a glance of myself at a strange angle. I watched myself as I freed my long silver hair from the nightcap. Old age creeps up in mysterious ways. My neckline was flush from the shock. I watched my forefinger in the mirror touch the red blotches spread.

Shadows among us, father would say, during a lightning storm. Huddled together by the fireplace, we'd watch the living room window cast shapely figures onto the walls. I walked down the hall to admire one of his favorite portraits. My fingers touched the paint strokes of a mother cradling her newborn, with her undying love. I remembered an old superstitious belief father once told me: mystic artists could capture the soul of the sitter in a single paint stroke. No wonder father never had his portrait done, with his mystical beliefs.

When I was young, I had to conform to society, religion, and family tradition. But now as a once independent, open-minded lady, I permitted myself these half-incoherent fantasies. The captain must have won a woman's heart. I touch my lips, remembering my Tom. My one true love of my youth.

I elbowed the mirror to polish a dirty spot and tightened my housecoat, admonishing myself for my ridiculous reaction to a simple left over from my dreams. I kneeled down to caress the red silk carpet runner on the oak floor that was in need of a hand wax polish.

I wondered if the future occupants would remove my father's worn rug and discard it for a runner that would be more fashionable. A Persian carpet perhaps as that seemed to be the new style. To me this old rug, like so many other things in this house, was a souvenir of father, but also like so many other things in this house, it was showing its age. I would keep an eye on the used furnishings and antique store up the street. Maybe this runner, and a few other things might end there. Leftovers from the public auction.

I thought about the captain's written legacy upstairs during my breakfast of hot buttered biscuits and tea.

Although I had the letter from the book in my pocket, I felt it more fitting that it should be opened and read in the attic room.

After I washed up, and put on a freshly starched house dress, I set off to retrace my steps of yesterday. There were other things to attend to in my last few days under this roof. But I felt an urgency to read this mysterious letter. I picked up my engraved silver letter opener from my writing desk. An initialized gift from Tom's parents. It was a memorable wedding present. Now, feeling fully prepared along with my flashlight, I marched on.

I know about fate. There's no escaping it.

That notion raced to mind and perplexed me. I thought about what I had read in the memoir yesterday. Both the captain's and mother's. The winding access was easier to maneuver this time round. I had become re-familiarized with the iron steps' unsteady ways.

After I walked across memory lane, packed to the brim, I was welcomed by an open door. My head poked in and looked around earnestly. The hawk's shrilling call jolted me out of my fantasy. From where I stood looking out, there was no nest on the nearby branches.

I went up to the glass to admire this majestic bird's mesmerizing deep red eyes. Its yellow and black talons were wrapped around the weathered ledge. Maybe it was on the lookout for intruders, or its a deliverer of a spiritual message. The thought rekindled fond memories of my childhood playfulness. Prepared with an open mind, I picked up the book from the chair, and settled into its place.

Captain, it pains me to know you left a well-deserved comfortable retirement in England for a lonely death under a Halifax wharf. No wonder I was not told your whole story as a child. I clutched his journal to my heart, knowing he had once held it as my nose twitched from a faint scent. It's that flowery perfume from the park yesterday. I set the book down on my lap. With Sally's childhood friend by my side, I slit open the envelope. I unfolded the paper, dreaming that the captain was watching me. I knew it!

The letter was a continuation of mother's story.

Life is a never-ending story.

She wrote....

I sent the children to their chores, then to bed without giving them the chance to open the chest. Somewhat half-asleep, I did that myself later that night after the storm. What I found surprised me, yes, but not as much as it might have, for I did know the captain and some of his story.

I hid it away, knowing not what I would do with it.

Charlie had straighten himself out. I would like to say he found the Lord, but he did not, rather he found himself. He sobered up and straightened up. It was the same day that the captain's chest came into our house.

Charlie got steady work keeping the books for a coal merchant, who bought the stuff from the Hub Shaft in Glace Bay. It was shipped south to Boston, and west to Montreal and Toronto.

I kept the trinkets from Charlie's last gambling adventure as a reminder of the bad times. And, in hope they would remind us how much better it was now, and ensure the bad times did not return.

Later, after the Provinces joined to form the Confederation of the Dominion of Canada—a more festive day there never was! My little Pearl Irene married Tom from up the road. I was proud of that and happy and sad. Tom was a good man, but a seafaring man, and I had seen what that would mean for my Pearl Irene. Anna married a man soon after, in the fur trading business, and moved out west with him.

My son Fred found himself work first on the docks in Halifax, and I am sad to say became a thief. He served time in jail for stealing a crate from a warehouse. I realized then what I must have known all along but never admitted to myself. Small things had been going missing from the house for some time. Nothing we would miss: a candlestick, or a comb, or a souvenir of the Queen's Jubilee.

When Fred was released from jail for good behavior, Charlie encouraged him to leave Halifax for a fresh start.

~~~~~

He left for the west. I gave him the trinkets to sell for a stake, to get himself started in a new life. I think he lost them gambling though. I guess that was fitting, seeing that's how we acquired them.

I had only one letter from Fred after, from Toronto, in which he said he was planning to move on to Winnipeg. I thought that he had maybe had another brush with the law. Rumor had it that he became a law-abiding citizen. That kind of gossip made me feel better. I do not really know what happened to him later in life, and it leaves a hole in my heart. But something in me knows he will be back on the east coast again, maybe in another life, but he will be back.

With no children left at home, and Charlie now working steady, we moved to Toronto with a letter of recommendation from Charlie's boss in Halifax, which secured him a position keeping the books for the city's largest coal importer.

Before we left, while packing our things for shipping them out west, I found the captain's treasure box, hidden down in the cellar. The time somehow felt right, seeing it buried under a mountain of old empty potato and onion crates. I opened it again for this first time since the day it was found. The statue was still there. The woman, pretty enough I guess, looking like some goddess from the history books with a carved laurel wreath.

~~~~~

I could not understand why the captain had hauled it around with him everywhere he went. Why he had kept it of all things when he had become so destitute that he could not even afford a sandwich or a bed for a night. I guess he truly was crazy. Anyway, I figured it had to have meant something to him, so I gave it to Pearl Irene's Tom, my eldest daughter. I thought that as the only seafaring man in the family, it might bring him good luck.

Though in retrospect, it did not seem to have brought good luck to the captain, and did not seem to do so for young Tom either. It was on his next voyage that Tom was lost at sea. My daughter became a twenty-year-old widow.

Now a diphtheria fever is eating at my body, my head aches, I have difficulty breathing, and the doctor tells me my time will soon be done. I write this letter for the captain's journal, that I found when I cleaned out his room in my mother's house. I had always kept it hidden under my bed. I wasn't sure why, but now I understand. Perhaps completing the story of his chest, or at least my part in it, will bring him, and me, some rest.

A few days later, with much of the house's contents already sold, and the few meager belongings Pearl could take with her was already moved to her modest room on Church Street.

Before handing over the keys, Pearl felt an urgency to make one last trip up the stairs to the attic. There was not much left in here either.

Pearl did find one item she had never noticed before. A portrait of a sea captain. She could not understand where it could have come from, surely she would have noticed it. The gilded frame was magnificent, and the painted likeness of a man so striking with his blue eyes. It was leaning up against the wall beside the window, where her inquisitive friend the hawk was again watching her, half-hidden behind the curtain.

That must have been it, she realized. The floor-length curtain had hidden it. Pearl had only saw it now because she felt compelled to pull the curtain further along its ceiling track, to where a sheet covering was crumpled up on the floor. This sheet was once Brizo's hiding place.

As she looked at the portrait, she became entranced with his longing. After all these years, it finally dawned on her. Pearl understood what Mabel meant by her words: whoever can finish the book will know the treasure's secret.

Pearl's face glowed with happiness, with each step that she took toward the portrait. She could hear the bailiff knocking, and eventually the door opening, and the heavy footsteps climbing the stairs below....

But she ignored that as her finger reached out.

When the eviction officer reached the attic, she was nowhere to be found.

- CHAPTER 15 -
Toronto, spring 2022

"Fred, don't panic, I can't talk now. Yes, my meeting is about to start." Tom's voice sank into a whisper. He was seated at the head of a boardroom table. "Noon? See you at Malcolm's. Yes, the same greasy spoon diner across from my office as last time. It's going to be a hectic morning. I had a disturbing night with little sleep. Later." The call ended with a fast finger swipe as his phone went into silent mode.

With his spiffy glasses in place, he cleared his throat. "Now to business, it's just past nine. Let's get started, shall we? The only way this partnership can move forward is if we can come to an agreement. Please pass me your proposal." Tom opened the sealed envelope before him. The morning hours went by as papers and chairs shuffled, followed by agreeable elbow and fist bumps, and laptops powered down. The deal was closed saving Tom's company for another few months as the last dulled sensation of the migraine lifted.

Tom admired his eyeglass frames and slid them into an inside pocket. He put his jacket on like a winner, patting his chest, thinking, *This amulet has brought me*

good luck after all. The sales specialist had assured him the metallic blue frames brought out the brilliance in his eyes. This edgy style depicts power and business savvy.

The revolving doors pushed him out of the office tower, and into a cold drizzle. Tom dodged slow-moving traffic as he crossed the street. Windshield wipers scraped away the half-frozen sleet as he ducked into Malcolm's diner. Without hesitation, he flung himself and his jacket onto the bench of a booth as the previous customers were vacating it. Tom warmed his hands under his breath.

Fred walked in a few minutes later with his shirt stretched across his stomach. He looked drained with a black boomer jacket draped over a shoulder. He stood in the open door looking for Tom in the crowded diner with its faded and stained 1960s mod wallpaper. He looked to his right at the chandelier that hung over a disused cashier's stall. It was a nostalgic display for the old timers, and forewarned of a cashless society in the future. To his left was a long counter with condiment baskets and napkin holders spaced out between the lunch plates. The regular patrons that were seated on the red vinyl stools looked over eying the door. They were annoyed by the incoming draft.

The door closed shut as Fred spotted Tom over the crowd. He made his way over and plunked himself down on the cracked vinyl bench. Being rundown was part of the place's charm. It was a landmark in the city's financial core for over a century.

~~~~~~

"You've got your usual table that's my Tom Adler. You're a regular now like those coffee-nursing patrons at the counter, glued to that flat screen TV. All they ever broadcast is breaking news with a stock market update."

"Look around Fred. There's lots of business people that'll be uneasy and irritable if ten minutes pass by without checking their portfolios. This place is always packed for a reason and it's not only the food. Big business deals are made on these sunken–in seats."

Fred picked up the glass of ice water and chugged it down. He wiped his chin with his sleeve then played with a sugar packet. "I don't understand how the fast food chains haven't pushed this diner off the block."

"I'm not sure about that Fred. They have an old hundred year city lease that expired during the height of the pandemic. The bailiff can come knocking any day. Builders are looking to buy the place and tear it down. Another anonymous glass tower with a multi-use complex is on the menu once real estate picks up again."

"Time will tell I suppose."

"What's going on with your mouth?"

"Oh, I was at the dentist." Fred went on. "Here comes root canal number two. It's scheduled for next month, not my idea of a fun morning. My mouth is still frozen from a small filling that needed replacing. I went for the package deal. I had a cleaning at the same time."

"The freezing will wear off, just watch your drool until it does."

"Got my message?" Fred tapped his fingers idly.

"What's up with Sally?"

"Glad you asked. Women baffle me.... I hope she was just over-reacting." Fred rested his elbows on the table. "Irene? Still seeing her, I hear she's special."

"Oh, she's incredible! What took you so long to introduce us? Now, about Sally, what happened? I can see you still care for her, that's a good thing."

Fred fiddled with his phone.

Tom looked at him, knowing it would be best to just let his friend talk. He knew where this was going.

"Couple therapy.... Oh you heard me right. I never fully got over the tragedy and loss of Anna. It was a heavy downpour that night, but, I was at the wheel and that blinding reflection in the windshield. The crackling sound of the splitting trees and those sirens!" He slurred the last few words. The numbness was giving way to a dull ache. "It's all in the past right? Sally insisted that I compromise and go to a few sessions together and try this new age technique to clear unwanted emotions away like this." Fred's finger tapped his left temple and then his right wrist and blew three times.

Tom smiled at his display of animated moves.

"OK, I'll think about it. A little tap here and there doesn't hurt, right? Oh, I was at the grocery store yesterday and I saw your wife with her partner ... really sexy couple. You never mentioned it."

"You mean my ex-wife. Let's leave that in the past too. I still need to work through it. It's still a raw wound as it caught me by surprise. We were married young with a long history together and adult children we both help out financially." He unrolled the cutlery from the napkin. Tom picked up his menu to change the subject. Fred flipped the menu stand over to see the lunch specials. He glanced up at Tom in surprise.

"You look ghostly, what's with the face? Plagued with a migraine again?"

Tom put on his jacket. He looked around suspiciously. His voice lowered into a tone of secrecy. "It's not the migraine ... I took my painkiller earlier on before my meeting. I had a strange experience that I can't figure out."

"Uh-huh. Do I know strange? OK. I can compromise on couple therapy but when it comes to my food...."

"Fred listen to me. It was more of a nightmare."

"Oh, do I know nightmares ... Sally also cleaned out my fridge when I wasn't home. She stockpiled it with healthy snacks as she calls it. Is this not nutritious food?" Frantically, Fred waved the menu in the air.

"She has your key? That's a first."

"That's history too after Sally threw them across the table." Fred rubbed his forehead trying to erase the restaurant scene. "Last week I went for my annual physical check-up.... Hmm, the salad does sound good though." Fred drummed his fingers as if to pause.

~~~~~

"Ready?" A voice announced with chewing pops.

"The all-day breakfast special: corn beef hash, three eggs scrambled with fried onions, bagel toasted, and a soda with a lemon squeeze." Tom's stomach gurgled. "Wait, hold the onions."

Fred got ready for the big decision.

"It's the diet special for this man. Malcolm's secret salad extravaganza, with a slice of whole wheat bread. Make that toasted, got it? And don't tempt me with butter and jam packets." Fred lowered his voice. "How about a creamy dressing with garlic and pickle bits?"

"This meal only comes with a low-calorie vinaigrette dressing. I'll put it on the side. Just water with your meal?"

Fred gave the thumbs up and the server left.

Tom tilted his head with raised eyebrows as a half smile swept across his face. Unable to make an excuse for his menu choice after the waitress had left, with arms flailing overhead, Fred blurted out, "I can't fool that face. My doctor gave me a fright. I'm close to borderline high cholesterol. He put me on a low-fat diet and said something about a stroke, if I don't watch it."

Tom stretched his legs out, his arms crossed over his chest. "A real diet, Fred? This calls for a celebration. It's a victory for Sally. Now you're watching your health, and not only the stock market."

"It's time I put my lifetime membership to good use. Looks like I'll see you around the fitness club. Sally told me you and Irene are working out a few times a week. Sounds like a plan for Sally and me." Fred paused to checked his messages. "Oh, looks like Margie wants to see you. It sounds urgent by her capitalized words and exclamation marks. Your phone must be on mute."

"Thanks for the reminder. I'm free all afternoon." Tom swiped his phone into ring mode.

Fred fumbled with his phone.

"Call her, apologize, Fred. Whatever happened, whoever said whatever, doesn't matter, just apologize. Sorry goes a long way. With Sally, I've never seen you this happy after all these years."

Fred thought about their romantic getaways.

"The usual without onions and the diet special." The server lowered their plates onto the table in front of them. Tom's fork was prepared for action.

Fred played with his salad. He knew Tom was right about Sally. He tried to figure out a strategy for his next move as if it were a business deal. Combined with the tempting smell of the beef hash was too much for him. His fork hovered over Tom's plate for a small taste, but Tom's fork blocked his.

"You're right, I'm a disciplined man, backing off now. Sally knows how to push all the right buttons. I have to hand it to her, I already miss her silly texts. Now, what's this about a strange experience? A nightmare? Sounds like an 18th-century novel: Tom Adler's Strange Experience." He dipped his toast into the salad dressing.

Tom's chin lifted up.

"Fred, look at me, I'm a total wreck. I acted as if nothing had happened last evening. But by the look on her face, I'm sure I didn't fool Irene at all. I suspect it has to do with this amulet that Margie gave me. Her cat Baster knows something about it. I know this sounds crazy, but I feel it in my gut."

Tom felt the room turn icy cold. He pulled his jacket in close. A fringe layer of frost was forming everywhere that only he could see. Tom's eyes went wild looking around. He started telling Fred the broad strokes of his experience with Baster's escape.

A voice boomed in his head: *Iris is her name.*

Tom slipped sideways off the booth bench onto the floor in shock. His head hit the ground and his fork flew across the room. He contorted and lost consciousness as the patrons watched in shock. He saw himself hovering along the ceiling, with his focus being drawn toward a log blockhouse with interlocking corners.

Tom was traveling into the past with the amulet pressed up against his heart guiding him. The heat from the wood-burning stove inside the building drew him in. He listened to the voices around the sparking cinders.

He looked around the room. It was a warehouse with a small window and a crowd of rough men. They couldn't see him beside them as he waved frantically for help. From the window, he saw a storm over a lake. Cries coming from under a trapdoor beneath his feet swung him around. His hand reached through the nailed planks that had faded into transparency with his touch. With a transparent hand, he felt the statue's iciness, but couldn't get a hold of her as his fist clenched with failure.

A fragrance breezed along the mosaic-style floor in the diner. A faint voice in his head plummeted him back into consciousness: *Iris, there's another way.*

Fred struggled to hold his flailing arms down as he gave a furious shudder before coming to. A woman shouted for someone to call 911 as the diner emptied out. No one was actually afraid, but no one wanted to get involved particularly with the COVID pandemic so recently tamed. People took public displays of ill health seriously.

Tom opened his eyes in excruciating pain.

"You blacked out, are you OK?"

"Iris?" Tom managed to sit up, with Fred's help.

"No, I'm Fred, your best friend on a diet. There's no Iris in your life that I'm aware of. Your girlfriend's name is Irene Montgomery. Do you want me to call her or maybe a paramedic?"

"I'll be fine." Tom's head rested in his shaking hands. "I don't have a history of seizures. My blood sugar level must have dropped. Maybe your lunch choice is a good idea. Help me up, I feel ridiculous on the floor."

"The show is over, move on." Fred told the few remaining patrons as their devices clicked away for dramatic social media selfies.

~~~~~~

"Ever since I met Irene, I've had bizarre experiences. Or, maybe I've lost it. Brain cells dying off from pills and downtown smog. It's too much for a suburbanite."

"There's always that chance too or age." Fred broke into a sweat babbling to distract Tom while he maneuvered him back onto the vinyl bench. "My grandfather was diagnosed with dementia just after he passed the century mark. Old age sneaks up on us."

The server brought over an ice pack and a hard peppermint candy for Tom. Fred held the ice pack on the back of Tom's head. He sniffed around. "Tell Irene to ease up on her perfume, it's overpowering on you."

"Irene doesn't wear perfume or make-up. She's a naturalist." Seated again, Tom came to his senses. Fred dabbed his own forehead with a napkin.

"I'm not sure what overcame me. All I remember is that I floated up to the ceiling. I watched myself sprawled out on the floor as a log frame building came into view, and...." Tom paused not ready to talk about the statue. "Everything around me turned into a white silence. Then I felt you holding down my shoulders. Maybe I hallucinated last night too?"

"Sure, whatever you say. Hmm, that's some whack you gave yourself. Here, take this, you know the spot better than me."

"Did you hear or see anything?" Tom put the ice pack on the bump. He crunched down on the candy. The ice and sugar soothed him.

"Hear? See? All I know is your cries made the hair on my head stand on end. You gave the floor a wicked beating. It was a cross between a horror movie and a kid's temper tantrum." Fred swung around whispering into his phone. He had left a message for his sister.

"Let's go! I've made a fool of myself."

"You know how to empty out a place."

The server waved the payment terminal politely over the table. "Credit or debit?"

"It'll be cash." Fred took out his wallet from his back pocket. "That'll more than cover it, and thanks for your help with my friend. Excuse me, please pack these to go. We have an urgent matter to attend to."

Fred carried the take-out boxes as they left.

Sally sat at the far end of the counter in a floppy hat and indoor shades. They always meet here when Fred needs a friend for sound advice. But, she never expected that kind of show with her meal. Wrapped in a cashmere shawl, she picked up the phone to call Irene.

The triple conjunction would soon be upon us. I feel Jupiter, Mars and Venus aligning in the heavens, with a bright comet fast approaching toward this solar system. It was from a neighboring galaxy that was called into action from the overseers of my sanctuary.

My story on this planet Earth would soon be ending.

- CHAPTER 16 -

Toronto, spring 2022

Tom walked hurriedly a few doors down the street. He turned the corner toward his hotel frazzled with what had just happened at the diner, and the memories of Baster's escape mixing, gave him a newfound fear of cats. He dodged around preoccupied pedestrians.

Fred caught up panting, and swung Tom around.

"Did you hear what I said?"

"Sorry Fred. I'm still a bit out of it." In a slower stride, Tom picked up the story of Baster's escape where he had left off. "I can't read her mind, but it felt like Baster had it all planned out. She must have suspected my night vision wasn't good. I was tripped by her leash on purpose to ensure my glasses would fall onto the ground. Maybe it's some kind of revenge for reprimanding her, or something. Then she escaped with my amulet. The thing's heavy too. How could she even have carried it?" Tom paused to catch his breath as his voice sank low.

"I chased her about two blocks toward a downtown alley. Then she veered left toward a construction site with a chain-link fence twice my height. Big signs were bolted onto the fence. They read: danger due to open excavation, private property, and caution electrified fence. Now, that's where I drew the line. I wasn't scaling a live wire fence, or let alone going into a construction site, or so I thought."

"So, she had a strategy to make life difficult for you. Maybe she's protective of Irene. A feline conniver that wants you gone."

"I wouldn't give her that much credit."

"She leaped over the electrified fence?"

Tom nodded nervously. "Even to recollect it, makes me shutter. I shielded my eyes from a security spotlight in the quarry as I looked inside. Something had overcome me. I felt compelled to follow her. By chance, I found a gap in the fence and squeezed in. It was then that I saw a huge creature on top of a truck as her amber eyes glowed toward me. It was surreal as if I was moving in slow motion backing away from the fence. Baster sat posed like a porcelain statue. A Sphinx, her ears erect, tail curled up around her side, casting a long shadow."

"How did you know it was her?" Fred was a bit uneasy.

"I saw the amulet clenched between her teeth. And there was an intense fragrance all around me. The same scent you detected at the diner. I thought I was the only one aware of it. Then she leaped at me with a shrilling scream." Tom paused to compose himself. "She knocked me down onto broken bricks. That's when I saw it."

"Err.... Saw what?"

There was an interval of silence.

"I didn't even tell Irene. It's even weirder than the giant cat, which could have been a vision thing, a trick of perspective, my imagination running away with me. But not this. We were in the pit, near the edge of the excavation. I could see the bricks and foundation stones of the old buildings that were demolished recently. And, I could see what looked like an exposed tunnel."

Tom's eyes sunk into a far-away look, thinking about the tunnel. "Baster came beside me shrunk down to her regular cat size again, before she headed into the entrance surround by broken and sharp debris. She stopped calmly and looked back before slinking into the narrow opening. It was like she was leading me there on a leash and I followed obediently."

"Oh, payback time. Go on...."

They had just reached Tom's hotel but Fred did not feel he could interrupt Tom's story, not after the episode in the diner. He wasn't even sure about letting Tom out of his sight for the next few hours, until he was sure his friend was all right. So, he followed him up to his room.

Tom washed up and put on a crisp blue shirt. With a refreshed appearance on the outside, he slipped his cell phone wallet into his shirt pocket. With his jacket on, Tom continued his story down the elevator. Fred only listened. They walked across the marble lobby and out the revolving door onto the crowded sidewalk. They were headed south toward the lake.

"I don't think the tunnel was long, though it was a tiring trek. The uneven passage was a mix of brick and stone and reeked of stale water. Even though there was no external light, the walls were covered in luminescent moss that lit up the passageway. It reminded me of the old catacombs in Paris, but not cleaned up. I think it went under the street to the bookstore where Irene works, where it ended. And that's where I found it."

"Found what?"

Tom looked around, not answering at first.

"When I got out of the tunnel, I took a better look at what was in my arms. It was a statue, about two feet long. It looked like wood but was way too heavy and too hard. It's shaped like some kind of goddess idol or something."

"Where is it?"

"I hid it outside the construction site. I didn't tell Irene. I don't know why. Then this morning while I was waiting for my new glasses, I took it to Margie's store and left it behind the planter with a note. It's there now."

"OK. That's your first good move."

"And last night, on my way back to Irene's building, Baster startled me with a loud meow asking me to pick her up like we were best friends. I looked down at her acting innocent. And she gave me back the amulet. Baster opened her mouth. It plunked down at my feet. Weird or what? That's when I saw Irene looking for us."

"Beyond weird. You're confusing me."

"You think you're confused? Fred, I keep seeing the thing, like it's alive. I saw it again or rather heard it trapped in that tunnel when I had that episode at the diner. I'm under too much pressure. Maybe I'm just losing it. I should speak to someone. I don't want to be a burden on Irene and make her into a therapist."

"Not a bad idea, the best of us can crack up." Sally came to mind, and their discussion about couple therapy.

"I questioned my sanity all night, wondering whether I had just imagined it all. And, I must have conjured up a hallucination of the statue during my blackout at lunch."

"You have luck on your side. You could have injured yourself much worse."

"Don't I know it! You said Margie wants to see me?"

"It must be about your statue."

"Let's go."

They made a fast turn toward the antique store.

A bell jingled as the door creaked opened.

"Anyone home?" Fred called out.

"It's always wonderful to see you. I was expecting you Tom, that was quite a surprise on my doorstep, fascinating find. I've just made a fresh pot of tea." Full of joy, Margie gave them both big hugs. "I'm so glad that you dropped by, perfect timing. Fred, I just listened to your voice message. No one is cursed."

"Good to know, just asking." Fred inspected the door. "What's going on here? Anyone could break in."

"Oh Fred, who would dare disturb my ghosts that roam after hours? They'll make sure the culprits are haunted for days to come. Besides, the security system would go off." Margie touched the loose hinge on the door frame. "I'll have the work crew add it to their to-do list. It must have happened yesterday. I had a crate delivered through the front door. It's the backdoor from now on." Margie picked up on Tom's discomfort.

"You look in pretty bad shape. What happened?"

"I've had the most bizarre experiences."

"He could be losing it from stress."

"Oh don't be ridiculous Fred. Tom, maybe it's your wish on the amulet? I had a strange dream about it." Margie recalled the memory as her smile widened, with a silver tray between her arms. "It's Mom's apple-almond tarts recipe, remember Fred? They had apples at the farmer's market. I couldn't resist the temptation."

"That was delicious Margie. It hit the spot." Tom recalled the wish that he made at the afternoon gala.

"Fred? You're not acting like yourself either." The aroma of the fresh-baked tarts triggered him.

"Don't try to tempt me!" Fred patted his stomach. "I'm on a reduction regime as my doctor puts it. Tea sounds good though, straight up please." He reached over for the cup. "Tom may need to watch his sugar level too. He put on quite a performance at the diner."

~~~~~

"It was if I was transported somewhere else."

"Oh Tom, mind-travel? How exciting!"

"Are you saying an out-of-body experience? If so, that sounds about right. I was shown something or I mean someone. I know it wasn't a hallucination. The statue's existence proves it. Right? Did you find anything out?"

"Oh, yes to everything, Tom. First, I researched the amulet from the pictures I had taken." Margie marched down the aisle to a quaint corner. She ushered him to sit down. Tom made himself comfortable on a plush velvet chair with gold rope trim. "I couldn't find anything in the worldwide museum database. It has literally billions of artifacts photographed most with meticulous details. Now, that in itself is extremely unusual."

Tom leaned in curious to hear more.

"But good news! We're in luck! It all changed in the wee hours of the morning. I had dreamed that I was thinking too narrowly, looking for a single origin, when there are in fact two." Margie sat down opposite him on a French style loveseat. "Relics like yours are extremely rare. It's authentic and one-of-a-kind." She patted the cushion and Fred sat down beside her.

"There, isn't that cozy? Just like old times." Margie shook his knee. "Now, where was I? Oh yes, the problem was searching for the amulet as a whole. It isn't all one piece. You see, what you have here is an extremely, unusual artifact."

Fred's ears perked up as his interest was stirred.

"It's like that cupboard over there beside the oval table?" Margie pointed at an odd cabinet that looked like two pieces stacked on top of each other, with a two-door cabinet on the bottom and the top with four drawers. "See how the wood is different between the two pieces, with different decorations. What you have is a French bottom cabinet from the late 1800s, and the top piece is a much older Italian piece. Sometime in the early 1900s. It makes a far more interesting piece this way. You would never figure out its provenience, I mean where it came from, if you don't realize it's two separate pieces. Your amulet is like that."

Tom pushed his analytical mind aside. He was open to a supernatural phenomenon explanation. Margie took some printouts out of a drawer. She placed them on the table. In the middle were pictures of the amulet. The other pictures around them had certain similarities to his amulet but none were entirely the same.

"The metal work seems to be Chinese. Ming Dynasty, 14th or 15th century. See this one here, and here?" She pointed to a picture with brass metalwork. Its design was similar to the amulet's frame. "But, instead of caging this bas-relief face in a small bottle, the carved stone was caged in a frame. The stone is probably ancient Egyptian ... look at this picture. So, what you have is a piece from ancient Egypt that found its way to China. Possibly a few hundred years ago, where it was placed into this brassy metal setting. And then, who knows what journeys it had to end up in this basement."

Tom recalled the wish made on the amulet again. He wondered whether he could possess supernatural powers by being in the amulet's presence.

"Tom are you listening? There are no coincidences if you can figure out the puzzle. You were clearly meant to hold it, at least for a while. Extraordinary, isn't it?" Margie sipped her afternoon cup of sweetened tea.

"Why would it want Tom, and say not me?"

"When the artifact declared itself, I just knew it was for him. Or maybe I should say through him to someone else, who knows. It must have been powerless downstairs, waiting patiently.... Anyway, enough of this fantasizing. Oh, your curiosity must be peaked about the goddess statue you brought to me. It was divine timing, her being an eternal persona. But, how she planned all this remains a mystery. I trust my instincts you know, my intuition. It appears you were meant to rescue her."

"Rescue? Who's in trouble?"

"Let her talk, Fred."

"She has an agenda like all of us, and the spirit world too. Now don't snicker Fred, it's true." Fred wondered if Sally had a plan too, and he hoped it included him.

"Folklore speaks of ancient relics that awaken under the right conditions. She's a statue that you found hidden in a recently excavated tunnel. In mythology, this may be part of her journey home. The stars had to align just so for this moment to arrive. Now, she's all cleaned up for her space travels. Ready to go home."

"Hmm, an exit strategy?" Fred declared quietly.

Margie bounced up from her seat and her zest startled both of them. "You must be curious follow me. We don't have much time, I have agents for a European buyer expected to arrive in an hour. They're always punctual."

She swirled a shawl over her shoulders. They followed her into an alcove at the far end of the room. "I'm sure it comes as no surprise that the statue you've unearthed is of a deity, with angelic-like features. She's charming. Maybe her coming out debut was last night, under the full moon."

"Say, when you first saw the statue, did you detect a perfume scent?"

"Yes, Fred, I did. Now that you mention it. Hmm, a little myrrh, rose, and cinnamon or something. It had a distinct aromatic scent, and it's still lingering a bit."

"You're right, it is...." Tom sniffed deeply. "I first started to smell it when Baster stole my amulet. The scent was overwhelming, where I found the statue."

"Who's Baster?"

"Baster is Irene's cat." Tom twisted his hands at the thought. "Actually, it might be some other kind of creature. Who knows. Baster gave the amulet back to me only after I followed her into the tunnel."

"I see.... The cat was drawn to the amulet's power." Margie's laughing eyes glistened, embellishing a mystical and comical-looking chase in her mind.

"Really?"

"Tom, felines are intuitive creatures. They have an innate sixth-sense ability. And, maybe there's a seventh ... even a tenth, too. How exciting! Now, amulets were mostly made for protection and some, like yours, may also contain the living essence of a mythological deity. Who knows what energies yours might hold? Baster followed her inner guidance and led you to her statue."

Fred interrupted excitedly, "Show it to Irene, Tom. Sally says she has a degree in anthropology."

"I'll do that, why not? At first I thought it was only a good luck charm. I'm sure she'll find it fascinating."

"Wait right here. I won't be long." Margie put a chiffon scarf over her beehive hairdo. With her faithful flashlight turned on, she felt like a heroine on her descent into the cellar.

"What's that noise?" Tom said.

"Need help?" Fred called out.

There was dead silence as they exchanged a glance.

"No, I'm fine!" Margie's voice echoed. "I can hear your mind chatter. There are no secrets between us in my underground hideaway. I'll be right up ... we're coming." Margie gathered her dress up. She cradled the statute under her other arm and brought it upstairs. Margie stood on the top landing with a victorious grin.

"Well, here she is!" Margie patted down her racing heart from the climb and the excitement of it all. "I had her in the basement to honor her privacy before her departure. She sure is a beauty all cleaned up. Let's go into my office." Margie entered first and placed the statue on the table beside the roll of drawings that had sealed the purchase deal.

"Who is she?" They said in unison. The afternoon sun cast a shaft of light over the upright statue. A luminous halo encircled her figure lending her a glow.

Margie touched Tom's shoulder. "I'm not sure yet, but you'll find out soon enough."

"What did you find out about her?" Tom was curious.

"First, where you found her. The construction site. It's only a couple of blocks from here near Khilto's. Here's a printout of an old land registry map from the late 1700s." Margie unrolled it on the table. "See this little dotted line?" Her finger floated over the spot. "That was a small creek running along Jarvis Street. It went past this store, under the construction site and Khilto's, and out to the harbor. In fact it shows Khilto's original foundation at the waterfront. It's been built out since then with landfill. Everything below Front Street is all artificial. In the 1800s, the railways needed land near the lake to build their tracks and necessary facilities."

"Margie, you're on a roll. Just look at how much the city has changed over the years." Fred looked down to check his phone. Still no messages.

"Yes, though lots has changed, this area is pretty much the same. Anyway I believe that the tunnel you found is a section of the old creek bed that was used as a garbage dump. It would have been easy for the city to make a storm drain out of it or a sewer. They used to do that, just run the sewage straight out into the lake."

"And this sewer or drain pipe runs all the way past here and under Khilto's?" Tom questioned.

"And, maybe it started much further north too. There's no way of knowing anymore. This is something you find in a lot of old European cities, such as Paris or Rome. It's only because Toronto is so young that we don't celebrate what is under our feet. Most of the antiquated sewer pipes had eroded and collapsed, or were filled in over the years. Though, when I realized this was what was out there, I took a closer look at the basement of this store. There is a wall that's built differently from the others, so it might have also been part of the sewer system."

Tom thought about the first time he saw Irene's laughing face. She was pulling apart a roasted marshmallow. "And I know there is some kind of weird basement at Khilto's, too. Irene had told me about a trapdoor near the coffee counter that was nailed shut for decades."

"That's enough about the tunnel. We'll never know how she got in there, but at least we understand where she was. Anyway, she's been there a long time. A century, maybe longer. That's important because it tells me she is not some modern fake, or at least not too modern. Now to the statue. First the material."

Margie handed Tom a jeweler's loupe.

"Take a good close look. See how it looks like wood, only with very tight rings? But it isn't wood, it is some kind of stone or metal. It looks more like Opal or Ammolite, or something with an iridescence allure. I'm not sure, but just look at how bright it is. In the dark it almost looks like it has a blue glow. So, some kind of stone but with a grain like wood."

"Petrified wood, maybe?"

"Possibly, but not a kind of petrified wood I have ever seen. Anyway. To the statue as opposed to its material. Doesn't this artifact's features look so real with a crystal in her brow? This is called the all-seeing third eye. The face on the amulet had one too. And, you're wish,Tom? Does it have anything to do with your recent experiences?"

"What about me, do I get a wish too?"

"Your wish has been fulfilled. With Sally! You two were made for each other, I don't understand why you broke up. Look at you, checking your phone every five minutes to see if she sent a text or something. Just call her. Now as I was saying, look right over here." Margie pointed out a hollowed area on the statue.

Before she said another word, Tom went from being perplexed and worried to flabbergasted. Almost speechless. "This amulet would fit in that exact spot."

"I believe this statute belongs to you, or at least it belongs with the amulet. You're the guardian of whoever she is. And, if a spirit possesses it, you'll find out soon enough. I've been an antique collector for many years. That's how these stories go. This seems to be a representation of the Greek goddess Iris. All the iconography is right, from her hairstyle and dress to the shape of her face. Look at her lovely enfolded wings with a caduceus by her side. All that's missing is her water pitcher. Tom go on pick her up."

This was all getting a bit too fantastical for Fred. He wandered back into the store's main room.

"This precious find is not a coincidence." Margie went on, ignoring Fred's disappearance. "I trust my instinct. I have a hunch that your encounter with Irene and Baster is not by chance either. Spiritual deities have a way of matchmaking for their own means. But it's almost time for my appointment."

Tom walked into the front room, with Margie right behind him. A French ormolu glass-paneled cabinet in the corner rattled as Tom looked around it. "So, there's a ghost in here after all."

"Why are you hiding in the corner?" Margie said.

"What about your diet?" Tom said.

I'm just waiting for a phone call, Fred signaled by waving his phone. He gulped down the last mouthful of corn beef hash.

Tom's hands tingled cradling the statue through the front door.

Fred followed as the agents brushed by them.

As the stone skips across the pond, I see a rainbow forming in the sky. Earth centuries have passed and my time has nearly come.

Thanks to Bastet's guidance of the mortal Tom, and Zephyr's more subtle manipulation of his friends, Fred and Margie, and all their entwined generations of lively appearances, popping in-and-out of reality's rippling pond.

The statue and the amulet will soon be united with my third spark that was lodged in the mortal, and the rifts it caused will eventually blend and ripple forth. The thin barrier separating no-space from the mortal realm has long since repaired into a reflective layer, and my place in the sanctuary awaits me.

- CHAPTER 17 -
Toronto, spring 2022

Sally and I met up for lunch the following week. She had left me a garbled message about Tom, and I was curious to find out what she wanted to tell me, but we couldn't get together any sooner. If it was news about our love life, it had to be given in person even if we had to wait to meet. It gave us the opportunity to look forward to a catch-up lunch taking advantage of the nice weather.

April arrived with the first warm spring day. Early blooming wildflowers poked out of last year's dead leaves in nearby city parks, and in the stone planters spaced out along the sidewalks. Birds chirped sharply, hidden in the budding hedges and treetops. The breeze from a pigeon swooping down under my nose, startled me. Its beak was aimed toward a half-eaten croissant near my feet.

In a plaid tweed jacket, I waited for Sally as people walked by in short sleeves and sandals defying Mother Nature. Winter was over in their minds. But there would be cold and wet days, and maybe more snow before the sweltering heat of a summer in the city, but no one was going to waste this rare burst of sunshine.

We met at a quaint French patisserie, that was only a short walk for both of us. Sally worked remotely, from home. She also went into the animation studio a few times a week. It was in a gentrified downtown factory converted into shared workspace. Her team needed the synergy of live brainstorming, as video platforms didn't provide the same creative momentum and productivity.

In front of the patisserie, I caught sight of Sally's wide-brimmed hat and belted floral dress as she came around the corner. She strolled carefree in the warm breeze under blue skies. The sight of her sky-high, red pumps touching down on the sidewalk, exuded her finesse and confidence. Was the thought of being graceful again only in my dreams or in another lifetime? My smile must have expressed my hidden wish. I waved her over, and we walked in together.

The place was packed. We swung our totes over the chair backs. There was a display case of croissants and pastries made on the premises, and posters of Renoir and Degas paintings decorating the fabric-covered walls. We sat down at the last table. The server stood over us with an order pad. "That's two sparkling waters, a fruit salad and an almond-apricot pastry for you, and a slice of quiche Lorraine and salad for your friend."

"Tom and I watched an episode of your queen bee show: Zeetumah. Fabulous animation, you're so talented. It's very cryptic entertaining scripting. How does your team think of such content?"

"That's storytelling. It's not easy to build a fantasy world with believable characters but it's sure fun to try. My creative juices really flowed on this project. I'm able to enjoy a lunch break without my phone binging every second, with panic texts and calls from the studio."

"I heard you broke up again. Did Fred lose it?" I spoke over the gossipy murmurs from the takeout counter.

"Actually, I did this time, in public. I'm still working through it. Our encounter was only a fraction of a second in the grand scheme of things. Life has its twists and turns at any age." Sally stumbled on her last words. She realized how much she cared for him.

"What happened?"

"We all try to change our partners to fit into our lives more easily. It's a natural process. You know what they say. A man marries a woman hoping she will never change, and a woman marries a man hoping he will, and both may end up disappointed. Most couples experience this and have to work through it together, or split."

The server brought over their lunch.

"We all need to adapt to a changing world, and how we relate to each other. That's why I suggested a method of couple therapy that introduces an energy healing technique that clears away deep-rooted habits and emotional triggers. I thought it was a great idea, for both of us. Fred was being Fred. I knew that he thought it was hocus-pocus by his demeanor. Well, I lost my cool, go figure."

~~~~~

"Hmm, I might try it, who doesn't have issues."

"I shouldn't have made a scene at the restaurant, but I was annoyed that he wasn't even listening to me. Fred pulled a toothpick out of his pocket and looked away. It was his way to disengage from our conversation." Sally finished up her quiche and salad.

"We've all been there."

"I appreciate our friendship. Thanks for understanding. It's only a timeout in my books. Have you noticed our lives have been so entwined lately? Freaky?" Sally flipped her long bouncy ringlets over a shoulder to re-apply her lipstick.

"Huh you're right."

"Fred hinted at moving in together."

"Oh so there's more to it. Commitment? Fred?"

"It was his idea but he got me thinking."

"Now you've peaked my curiosity."

Sally mimicked zipping up her smile with a finger.

"OK. Got it! What's the news about Tom?"

"He met Fred for lunch at the diner last week. You know the place, Malcolm's across from his office? Tom threw himself onto the floor. His arms flailed wildly, and it looked like he was trying to grab the air. Maybe a seizure? I saw him speak, but I couldn't make it out from across the room."

"Oh, my!"

~~~~~

"It lasted less than a minute and then they left. They both looked overwhelmed. Fred didn't even notice me at the counter by the door. I have to admit it was upsetting."

"Tom never said a word about it. He must be embarrassed." I scooped up the last spoonful of fruit salad. "I know his life story, but he never talked about his mental state other than that he was stressed from the business and the divorce. But who isn't stressed these days? I hope it's not serious. It's as if he's hiding something. This probably sounds crazy but I think Baster knows what it is."

"Baster, your cat?"

"The jury's still out on whether she's a cat, but yes."

"Seriously?"

I hunched forward with a nod.

"Anyhow, I thought you should know."

"You were at their favorite lunch spot?"

"OK, I spied."

"Better than stalking him on social media."

"Oh, I almost forgot. Margie, Fred's sister, gave Tom an ancient amulet a while ago. That was some gift, so I've heard. I'm curious ... have you seen it?"

"No, he never mentioned it."

"It's obvious he needs a secret good luck charm."

"We all have secrets by our age."

"About my visit to the diner, let's keep that a secret."

"My lips are sealed!" I mimicked Sally's finger zip from earlier on. "You have my word. Oh, good news, Tom has planned a road trip, and Fred may join him."

"That's a great idea for both of them. Fred really does need a break from his work. It's been a challenging fews years in the financial sector. Business closures, restructuring...." Sally raised her water glass for a clink-clink to our friendship. "Where are they going?"

"Tom did one of those DNA tests, where they reveal all your ancestry. Well, it also identified some long-lost relatives out east, in Nova Scotia. Second cousins or first cousins once removed or something. I never understood all that stuff. Anyway, they were in contact by email. It developed into a friendship. They invited him to come visit this summer."

"That will be good for them. As long as Fred stays away from cliffs!" Sally laughed. She recalled what the fortune-teller had told him, and the look on his face. "Summer is around the corner. There will be kayaking on the lake, street festivals and outdoor patios with music until dawn. Romantic evenings as the city comes alive after dark. I hope Fred is a part of it with me."

"Maybe we'll have a double wedding after all. Remember how we giggled about it at overnight camp?"

"Good memory Irene, that's a lifetime ago."

"Oh, speaking of that reader at Khilto's, Tom went to see her at the store. Fred had encouraged him to go after his experience. Tom was curious about his future."

〜〜〜

"How fun for him."

"Not really, it was a big mistake! I wasn't there but Tom told me everything as if it was a confession. He had shuffled the deck, cut the cards, and handed them to her. Then, once the cards were laid out on the table, she went hysterical on him as her fingers flailed wildly, decked out in flashy rings."

"Really?"

"Tom went on to say she refused to tell him anything as she gathered up her things early, and returned his money with an apology. She dashed out the door saying there was a client emergency that she forgot about. It was embarrassing for him as the patrons at Khilto's looked on."

"He's had a lot of weird experiences recently."

"Yeah, but he's not the only one." My mind wandered to the last entry in my journal.

"I hope this is the end of it for both your sakes." Sally acted silly probably thinking that I was only joking. She excused herself to go the to washroom.

I thought of the tandem bike with a big red bow. The elevator wasn't working again, and Tom had to lug it up the stairs with his sore back. It was a surprise for me. I never want to fail him. I haven't told him yet, but I may be a candidate for the latest solar powered technology in hearing aids without surgery. This nearly invisible device has a sound processor that fits behind your ear, and it's not chunky.

Maybe one day I can reclaim my career as a soundscape maestro. Why not? I'll recreate my destiny in the process. I'll be the best attuner the world has ever heard. Melodies as beautiful as the music of the celestial spheres in the universe, that inspired all of the great composers. The possibility excited me as I envisioned our future together.

Sally's hand rested gently on my shoulder, jolting me out of my wishful thinking. With a smile, I crumbled up my napkin and gave my watch-face on my wrist a quick finger tap. "Time goes by fast. I'm glad we had this time to catch-up."

"Irene, let's do this more often. It's always fun."

We split the bill. With gestured kisses smacked in the air, the door swung shut in the early spring sunshine.

～～～

The three-planet conjunction and the elliptical orbit comet, are now in the morning sky to lend the energy I will need to make the transition. The two vessels with the fragments of my self, the amulet and the mortal Irene, were together once more. I had bewitched Tom to leave me on the windowsill in his hotel room, overlooking the construction site where he had found me.

Close enough. I can take it from here.

My return to no-space will leave a wake of damage that'll ripple into the Age of Aquarius. The cause of drifting

～～～

tides upon the lives of the mortals around me was a mishap on the water's surface. But such wounds heal, as humanity has learned to adapt to changing tides and bubbly mishaps, ever since invisible deities influenced this world with its rhythmic cycles.

And anyway, there is no escaping fate.

- CHAPTER 18 -

Toronto, April 2022

Yesterday afternoon was a dramatic scene on the kitchen floor. The breakfast nook and counter-tops will never look the same to me again. Soon after our intimate escapade, the atmosphere changed rapidly with the Ouija board episode, and the amulet later on. I was looking at the pizza box near me, as I had begun to doze off, when the alarm sounded 8:45 PM, alerting me of my 10 PM shift at Khilto's.

With less than a few hours of rest, Tom was a wreck, as I reflected back on him. Flabbergasted, he admitted to being pulled in-and-out of a nightmarish dream of being chased down a never-ending tunnel. My lucid dream was a surreal out-of-body experience.

Now, walking home from my midnight shift, mulling over the sequence of events for the umpteenth time, I realize that the dream that came to me, as I tossed and turned beside Tom, was the exact same vision that I had witnessed when I first applied for the job at Khilto's. I am at the same location where I had first crossed paths with Baster.

Years ago, I used to take pain medication that could give me flash illusions. But, this wasn't the same. It was a desperate cry for help. Someone was trapped in a tunnel. The voice had a rhythmic tone to it. But, it wasn't a cryptic message.... It was a forewarning. This sounds ridiculous even thinking about it. I must tell Tom about this. He finds my spiritual rationale humorous.

I carried on home.

Oh yes, as for Tom's weird behavior. He must have blacked out yesterday, that's all. I recalled what Sally had told me about the scene at the diner last week. Perhaps it was a seizure. He could have had a concussion from the fall. That's why he was acting so animated.

Anyway, he never mentioned this incident to me. Or, maybe Tom has epilepsy or some other hereditary neurological issue. He's taking some medication I wasn't aware of. I knew there had to be an easy explanation. That's why he did the DNA test in the first place. I'm sure he has other secrets too, who doesn't? None of my business, I suppose. Though, if he were serious about me, he would mention it.... Wouldn't he?

I paused.

Yesterday with the Ouija board, hmm, maybe I was pushing the pointer around the board, guided by my subconscious spelling out my birth name. That's it!

I had only weaned myself off anti-anxiety drugs early last spring. Although it was a low dose, I had experienced the occasional abstract fleeting thought. It was a known side-effect. So, nothing supernatural happened: we just played the game after an early dinner and caught a few winks of sleep. That's all that happened. Why is my mind racing non-stop? I had to forget about it or I'd drive myself crazy.

Tom had told me last night that the amulet was meant for me, and that it was a surprise. I had looked into his eyes for any clues, but he seemed sincere with his words. We both got ready to leave: him to his hotel room and me to Khilto's.

Then I was puzzled by what he said next: "Oh, about this parlor game, what a waste of time, it doesn't work. I'll get rid of it at a second-hand store." I was shocked by the way he picked up the board waving it "good-bye" in the air. "We need to obey the game rules. Did you forget?" Hmm.... Tom was so casual about it and dismissed it so lightly.

"My road trip's all set. I have long lost relatives to visit out east. Fred will be joining me. We leave in about three weeks. The weather should be warm enough. No more risk of spring snowstorms." Tom had told me about his plans and left. He went to catch a few more hours of sleep in his hotel room.

My mind drifted to a flashback of me standing in front of the hallway mirror with the amulet's eyes facing me. It really does feel like it was meant for me, even if Tom wanted to be silly about it. But he meant well, I was sure of it. What would I do without him? He's an answer to a prayer.

~~~~~

This is ridiculous, it's taking forever. I turned my wrist over to see the time. What? Forty minutes had passed since I locked up Khilto's. I should have been home long ago. It's only a ten-minute walk, fifteen tops.

The glistening array of predawn stars captivated me. The fierce, gusting wind swept a brief clearing in the storm clouds. What? I could see Venus and Jupiter almost touching in the sky, and was that Mars right beside them? It made me realize that decades have passed since the astrologer had prophesied my future.

My destiny couldn't possibly have anything to do with Tom, could it? The predication had warned of a midlife crisis, was it his? Were the stars in position calling for me? I could not tell as the eastern sky was already brightening, and the fainter stars were becoming lost in the growing light. I whispered to what looked like a shooting star streaking across the morning skies.

A comet?

That must be it. My destiny has come, I half joked. The idea distracted me only for a second. An uneasy feeling was brewing up inside me. With my hand over my heart, I inhaled slowly managing to calm the onset of sheer fright. My panic attacks had started after I watched our family home burn down with all my childhood memories. I had learned breathing techniques to help control them. No more pills I told myself. I can do it. I clutched the strap of my tote.

This last shift hadn't been easy on me. A teenage gang was prowling around outside Khilto's in the alleyway, and it rattled my nerves when they peered into the window to watch me.

In this neighborhood, the downtown streets attract a diverse crowd after the restaurants and clubs locked their doors. I felt vulnerable to even leave the premises without the sun in the sky. Instead of a supernatural being, was it one of the thugs waiting for me in the shadows?

I swung my head in every direction. My instincts warned of impending danger: I was not alone. My legs buckled right from under me. I hit the ground with such force barely missing the concrete traffic barrier. Startled by the echo of construction scaffolding crashing down, I think I still managed to lift my head. Maybe a bit? Now that was unexpected. I'm careful on broken asphalt.

With my toque tugged over my ears, I had an epiphany. An awakening? I had a strong sense this fall had already occurred with the same earth-shattering intensity.

There's that déjà vu feeling again. I looked around from street level. No one was there but the sight of blood on my scuffed hands fed my rising panic. My shattered wristwatch was lying on the pavement beside me. It read 7:05 AM. What? A minute earlier it had read 7:45 AM. It now showed the exact moment I had left Khilto's. That's not possible! The watch hands must have flung back on impact, I convinced myself. It's only a crazy coincidence.

〜〜〜〜

What are the chances of that happening? I'll have to tell Tom about this too, it's unbelievable. What a fiasco this morning. Now, if I could cradle my knees, the throbbing might stop. My favorite jeans are probably torn and not in a fashionable way.

When I was a child, mother would gently pick out the gravel from the open wound. I remembered how my scraped knee once tingled in the cool air after I fell from my bike. "Here's a tissue from my purse my dear, now place it over the boo-boo." I heard my mother whisper softly in my hearing aid, then she kissed my tears away. The stinging subsided in my mind.

The heavy clouds burst open. Large raindrops splatted down, stirring the city soot, as lightning flashed behind the buildings. The odor of ozone soothed my racing thoughts. It wasn't a good week for accident-prone me, I can handle it. Life seems to be getting better. I thought of Theresa's face when she first met Tom.

The lamppost cast an odd, grayish shaft of light on a trashcan that had crashed down against a telephone pole. My eyes rolled over toward a screeching cat that had jumped off its lid. Otherwise, the street felt more empty than usual. There should be a city work crew milling about that corner by now. I heard the muffled honks and drowsy sounds of morning traffic in the distance.

This was where Baster had led Tom on a merry chase, I mused, and that Toronto is the crane capital of the North American dream. A city in transformation with massive towers. But each tower had a deep underground, scooped from the clay and blasted through the rock exposing the layered geology and history of the city. I watched mesmerized as another section of scaffolding over the sidewalk, toppled in the gusting wind.

I'm numbingly cold and that prickling sensation is becoming unbearable. I can't reach out and touch my leg. It's lying in such an awkward position that I find funny. How is that possible? My body is weighing me down. Every effort I make to try and lift myself up, I can't, just can't.... I'm not going anywhere.

This is ridiculous! I hear myself think. What is that writhing movement inside my chest? It's annoying me too as I can't reach out and calm it down. I think I've shifted my head barely enough to see through a section of the collapsed scaffolding. What's that?

A buzzing sound pierced through my ears. I imagined covering them with my palms to block it out. Soon it softens into a dull hum. I should scream, but I can't do that either over the noise of more scraping metal falling, covering me. I wish my chattering mind would stop.

The morning light deepens into a brilliant silver sheen around me. Its startling presence brings a wave of calm, as I realize that I am feeling detached. Indeed, detached is the only thing I am feeling. I can no longer feel my legs, or arms, or body, or even my head. It must be close to eight o'clock by now. Baster is probably annoyed that I'm late. I'm going to have to change my plans this afternoon. I'll need the sleep. Somebody will walk by and help me up. I'm feeling ridiculous lying around. It's totally frustrating.

I had watched my tote bag plunk down hard into a puddle and everything spilled out. The splash had set off cigarette butts to float toward their destiny in a sewer drain. I hear myself think about nonsensical things, as the dawn broke through the clouds. My attention was drawn up to a magnificent rainbow. The colors are the most glorious colors I have ever seen in the dawn sky.

Is this an omen?

Or, is it the sign the astrologer talked about?

A tall shadow is moving toward me, but I can't make out any features. I can't move my head to look at it straighter and as it gets closer, it passes outside my vision, to my right. I knew it all along.... It was following me from the alleyway.

Who's there? I try to ask as the shuffling sound stops. I feel its presence as it kneels down beside me and touches my heart. My eyelids feel heavy. I can no longer keep them open, as I lie helpless under the debris.

The reality sets in: I am dying.

I see ribbons of light swirling out from of the rainbow's crest above. They twirl into a flowing script. I can make out the message through a silver sheen that cocoons me, enveloping my body in a brilliant light. It is my name in ancient Greek letters and Aramaic, then in Latin, and finally in Egyptian hieroglyphs.

I can read them all.

I realized: I was born Iris. There was no escaping fate, by simply changing my name. A strong westerly wind sweeps over my wayward hair matted with blood.

Tom have I failed you? I thought I had whispered.

Iris. It is time.

Yes, I'm Iris ... Tom I love you ... please don't leave me. My thoughts are no longer clear enough for even me to hear. A thunderclap in the dawn sky rocks the city and the wind dies down. My shoulders rise up separating from my motionless form. Muffled sounds of the city waking up fade out.

The luminous sunray lifts me higher and higher.

This life fizzles out in white static.

I am gone.

The bell in a downtown church steeple struck eight o'clock. Morning traffic hummed by, and the work crew got on with their morning. Irene never made it home after her shift.

A construction scaffold crashed down, and her body lay motionless under it on the sidewalk. The astronomical event occurred as Mrs. Delos had predicted decades ago. Irene's essence was now at peace amongst the stars. She was a starlet waiting for her next window of opportunity, to cast her self into an earthly experience once more.

Influenced by the celestial coordinates, The goddess now had the power to reunite her three disparate parts.

Eyes of stone glistened with a blue glow as thin lips widened on the amulet. It had fallen off Irene's neck and onto the sidewalk, as the spark of Iris that it had sheltered, floated out in a luminous light strand. And, the ancient Chinese artifact returned to the sandy shores of Oyster Secret in the year 1421, fulfilling its purpose.

At the same moment, the stardust energy of the goddess separated from the incarnate being, and the statue in the hotel room also gave up her essence, turning from stone back to wood. It decayed instantly to the sawdust it would long ago have become if the goddess' essence had not preserved it.

A glowing orb flashed across the skyline.

Regally, goddess Iris had left the physical world to return to her place on the other side of the rainbow as blue Irises blossomed across Allan Gardens in her wake.

From up above, I watched as Death took Irene Montgomery, and her Earthly consciousness vaporized into the ocean of consciousness. I gazed through the stuff worldly dreams are made of in her ruling constellation of Aquarius in our starlit universe. Its stardust is the emotions all living things.

As Jupiter moved out of alignment with Mars and Venus, the comet's tail faded out, and the Zodiac dial turned into its next position, closing my star gate crossing home to no-space. It was a window of opportunity, and I took it.

My golden-hued irises looked through the blue veil that separated the higher and lower worlds. I could hear the echo of Irene's phone ringing inside her tote, as distracted people on their devices walked by dodging the debris from the windstorm, not even looking close enough to see the human form lying beneath it all.

A construction worker, rounding the corner, found the collapsed scaffold and saw the form beneath it. Moments later sirens wailed as the world continued its course through the heavens, scarcely marking this tragedy.

≈≈≈

- CHAPTER 19 -
Toronto, October 2023

It was early autumn. A turquoise sky dome set the ambiance for daybreak. More than a year had passed since Irene's tragic accident. Their short-lived romance had left an indelible impression on Tom. He tried to blot-out her tragic ending but couldn't erase even the most minute detail of her memory. Deep inside, he knew their ties were not severed. Still, he carried on.

Both, he and Fred had planned their road trip the previous spring but had postponed it because of Irene's tragedy, and the unfolding events that followed after her passing. Now, with the initial impact of the pandemic a fading memory, and the economy was more or less back to normal, they decided now's the time as this opportunity may never come around again.

His great grandmother on his mother's side, Anna Thompson, was one of three siblings that had lived on an island off the Village of Chester, in Nova Scotia. Her mother had grown up in Halifax, and that house, now a Bed & Breakfast, was still in the hands of descendants of one of her children. His distant relatives had invited him to come stay for a week and renew family ties.

242 | JULIANNE BIEN

Tom had plenty of time to figure out how to fill that huge order. He knew it would come to him on the Trans-Canada Highway. He looked at Irene's number, still in his contact list. His finger hovered over her name to delete it, but he wasn't ready yet.

Irene had no living relatives so he looked after her funeral arrangements, closing all her accounts and liquidating her assets. All the proceeds went to the Royal Ontario Museum's endowment fund. Her clothing was donated to a women's shelter. He knew that would have been her wish. However, Tom kept her journal about the captain as it had intrigued him.

With his suitcase in the trunk, Tom placed his device in the phone mount beside the gearshift. His curly man-bun, grown since Irene's death, exposed an earring stud. Theresa had picked out his birthstone for it when she persuaded him to get the piercing.

"Hey Adler," shouted a neighbor, "have a good trip, you deserve it!"

"Thanks, it's long overdue. I almost had a breakdown being forced to declare bankruptcy so soon after the divorce, and well … everything else. But, post-pandemic is all about reinventing yourself, right? New leaf, first day of the rest of your life, all that stuff. This business endeavor is doing better than my old one ever did."

"Who could have seen it coming? Lots of businesses didn't make it through the crisis. You were not the only one. But you sure bounced back. Never thought you'd become an App Developer, with a space travel theme."

~~~~~

"That's how I was able to finance this place."

"You have incredible ingenuity. Where's Fred?"

"I'm on my way to pick him up. Get this … his fortune-teller from Khilto's is now his business coach. She had forewarned him of this massive shift in the markets. The cards saved him from financial ruin."

"Isn't that the same reader who told him to stay away from cliffs last year?"

"You're right! I totally forgot. Probably because I tried to forget my own experience with her."

"The east coast has plenty of cliffs."

"I'll keep him safe, no worries. Keep an eye on my place while we're gone. Here's a spare key if you need it. You know, if the roof caves in. Or, there's a mass flooding from burst pipes on the street."

Tom pushed a button on the dashboard as the trunk's lid lowered. It locked with a familiar click. The crisp air on the cloudless morning, invigorated him. Tom squinted from the glare of the polished red hood. Theresa had picked out this sporty convertible with tan leather seats for him. Close in age, she knew how to manage his midlife crisis like an expert, especially after the tragic loss of Irene.

"I'm here for you buddy. Have a safe trip."

"Stay out of trouble!" He revved up the car and drove off. The grinding gearshift of his sporty car sent a flock of birds into flight from the maple trees on his front lawn. A breeze rustled the withered leaves across his driveway. Memories flooded in. It was almost two years ago during the pandemic, when he had first met Irene, and his crazy incident with Baster.

The red convertible pulled over in front of Fred's luxury building, overcome by emotion as he recalled the sirens from the morning Irene died. Tom had gone over to her place and let himself in. He planned on surprising her with roses as an apologize for his antics the previous evening. He had looked out her window at a row of police cars and an ambulance, turning the corner down the street. Never in his worst nightmares did he think that it might be for her.

Distracted by a honking horn behind him, Tom pulled into the driveway. He sent Fred an arrival text, then thought again about that crazy spring as he waited for Fred to come down.

First, there was the statue Baster had led him to, that Margie said was of the goddess Iris. It was stolen from his hotel suite. The hotel manager insisted that the digitized door lock was never opened after he left. Tom never believed him. All that was left was a small pile of sawdust on the windowsill, though no one could figure out where it came from.

There was no indication of forced entry, and nothing made of wood was damaged. The statue was a valuable artifact, and it was missing, and in Tom's books that meant stolen. That's how he reported it to the police, anyway.

~~~~~~

His bereavement therapist said to forget about it. It was probably an inside robbery, and the illusion at the diner was induced by stress combined with the bad fall, that was due to slipping off the vinyl bench onto a wet floor. He never had another episode, and the doctor Margie eventually made him see could not find anything wrong with him. There were no indications of a concussion on the brain scans.

The thought of Irene's cat still made him uneasy. As his therapist had suggested, he started voicing his thoughts out loud to tame them, and give himself the perspective to examine them more rationally.

"Baster disappeared the same day. The crazy part is that it didn't come as a surprise to me, it was like I expected her to be gone," Tom aired, fidgeting with the steering wheel. "Those amber eyes still gives me the chills." Through the condo's glass doors, he could see Fred stepping out of the elevator with Sally laughing in his ear.

"One thing I couldn't figure out was that the amulet was not on Irene when she was found, nor was it in her home. I have a strong suspicion that Baster stole it. But, there was no way to prove it. And that creature's probably still lurking in some downtown alleyway."

Fred was wearing retro goggles, and a driving scarf, looking like something out of the Roaring Twenties. Traces of his breakfast were visible on his sweater.

Sally waved and shouted out pleasantries from the manicured garden entrance-way. Tom raised a hand, and gave her a good-bye salute. They had become engaged three months ago. This road trip was to be Fred's last adventure as an unmarried man. It was a substitute for a bachelor party.

Fred marched proudly over with a large roller suitcase. "We're looking forward to our double wedding with you and Theresa next month. An outdoor celebration, with your gazebo for the ceremonies is auspicious, so says Margie. Oh, she's in charge of the caterer and decorations. You know my sister."

"Looks like we're both doomed, my friend. This is round two for me. Throw your suitcase in the trunk. The back seat is reserved for the healthy snacks and cases of water." Tom swung around, pointing over the seat at the twin coolers tucked into the narrow bench that passed for the sports car's back seat.

"I hope this stash include some pepperoni sticks and chips." Fred sank into the seat and put on his seatbelt.

"It's hard to believe we're making this happen." Tom pushed a button as trunk's hood lowered with a quiet hum. "Three days driving to get there, a week with my relatives, another week exploring museums and historic sites in the Maritimes, then three more days to get back. The Internet makes the world a smaller place, but it sure doesn't shorten the drive."

"Don't I know it! I can't believe Sally encouraged me to go. The east coast is in my blood too. My fortune-teller was right. She hasn't let me down yet. We were destined for this trip."

"Well, you wanted a midlife adventure before you tied the knot and here we are doing it together. Sally really helped you accept the truth that the tragedy wasn't your fault. It's been decades since your fiancée died in a car accident. You never were a jinx to her by just being engaged. Anyway, how's your sister?"

"More good news! She became close to Sam, her friend the real estate broker, ever since the portrait of her sea captain and his woman was stolen last year. That's a mystery she'll never let slip away. She'll figure it out with Sam someday. Seems he always wanted to design security systems for museums. So, he's going crazy with the security for her store. They're considering moving in together, but you know my sister."

"This trip will be good for both of us, and for Sally and Theresa too. They'll get a chance to finalize the wedding plans without us around." Tom pressed on the gas pedal with his new limited edition sneaker and revved the engine. "Theresa helped me furnish my townhouse. She'll be moving in when we get back. Fred, she sure is fashion conscious."

"I can see!" Fred spiraled his finger at Tom's bling and designer jeans. "Don't go overboard with the man jewelry. Remember your experience with that amulet?"

"Don't remind me, I'm trying to leave the past where it belongs."

"You had luck on your side and talk about timing. Good thing Irene had introduced you to Theresa when you picked her up after her shift. She was concerned about Irene when she didn't show up at work. She was clever to have tracked you down at the diner."

"I remember my first date with Theresa. I had one condition if she wanted to see me again."

"What was it?"

"That she'd never ask me to take her dog for a walk."

"Smart thinking, good move." Fred chomped into an apple as if to agree. He never fully understood what had happened with Baster that night at the construction site, but it had clearly scared his friend.

"Yeah, thanks to Irene, I met Theresa. I'll never forget Irene's quirky bursts of laughter when I would surprise her at work."

"Let's top it up before we get out of the city."

"You've master the talent of mind-reading?" Tom twisted the wheel to the right and stepped on the gas, suddenly feeling unhinged from the memory of a street scene: Irene's glassy-eyed stare the night of Baster's sinister plot.

Tom pulled into the gas station near the highway on-ramp. He also had the transmission and tires checked by the attendant. Fred took advantage of the pit stop. He added some beef jerky and a six-pack of root beer to their snack collection.

~~~~~

Motel nights and days of driving passed on the Trans-Canada Highway, eastbound to Nova Scotia. They took a scenic route, and during the Quebec segment, Fred insisted on a couple of stops for authentic Poutine: French-fries topped with cheese curds and gravy. When they reached the Bay of Fundy, Tom pushed a button to lower his smart roof. It was nearing the end of a beautiful, sunny day with a stiff ocean breeze.

Later that afternoon under a rapidly graying sky, Tom pulled over behind a billboard advertising the best lobster rolls in the Village of Chester. He wanted to raise the roof. The breeze had turned to violent gusts as dark clouds crept in from the horizon.

"What's that?" Fred took off his sunglasses to look out into the high tides. Startled, he grabbed onto the dashboard to steady himself.

Frustrated, Tom recalled what the statue told him at Irene's condo that fated afternoon. He gripped the clutch as her face filled the windshield through a blue veil. With a lifted finger her familiar words rippled through him in a voice he had tried to forget: *It is a match made in heaven but in another ripple.*

"Whoa, that's crazy!" It was the same cryptic message that I had heard the last time I saw Irene alive. The wind picked up force. The satellite radio sizzled out and the dashboard controls dimmed out. The goddess was gone and the ignition shut down abruptly.

An electrical storm had moved in, blackening the skies, and slashing their retinas with lightning flashes. Tom pounded on the wheel of his spiffy car that had failed him. Freaked out that he was seeing things again.

"Yes, it's crazy all right! This is not the place to get stranded with the top down." The seagulls took flight overhead, their shrilling cries made Fred wince. He reached over to the driver's side blasting the horn into one long siren to scare them away.

"The car won't start." Tom faced reality. He grabbed his phone to call for roadside assistance. The black screen lit up with crackling lines as it dilated into a blue puddle that spread across the screen. It turned into ice. Frantic he watched the words etch into it: there's no escaping fate. He flung the phone far as it crashed onto the rock and was engulfed by a mounting wave.

"Wasn't that a bit extreme?"

"Is yours working?"

"No bars for the boss. Whoa that's jail talk my boy." But, Fred was only half-jokingly. Those words felt eerily familiar for some reason. Tom searched the glove box. He pulled out the owner's manual. There had to be a procedure for raising the top manually.

"It only refers to the automatic features, it's definitely not user friendly. It says nothing about a sudden shutdown of its computer system. Oh, here it is ... call your local dealer. OK, will do. This is not useful!" Tom shouted sarcastically and got out of the car. He managed to pry open the electronic hood by hand. A penknife is a handy backup gadget.

Fred fought with the wind and looked over Tom's shoulder. He held up his no-service phone to shine a light on the engine ... not that it would help in a storm. Tom looked up, neither of them knew the first thing about automobile repair.

"Fred, good news, free vehicle during repair this once said." Tom held up the soaked manual that tore apart in his fingers. The crashing waves against the rocky shore were hypnotic. The torrential downpour kept them shifting on their feet as if a change in position would stabilize them. The gulls had disappeared to safety.

Tom looked up at Fred's cry.

"Look!" Fred's cupped hands shielded his face as he watched on. A lightning bolt had struck the ocean with fury. Massive waves peeled away exposing a masthead rising up from the water's depth in a cloudy mist. "Tom, a sunken shipwreck has surfaced before our eyes. We have unbelievable luck. What an adventure!" Fred forced himself to step out onto the cliff's edge for a closer look.

Tom grabbed his arm. He cried out to stop him. They both slipped on the huge rocks. The storm had stirred up a tornadic-funnel. The huge waterspout moved inland at incredible speed, veering toward the rocks where they stood. Fred was drawn toward the vanishing ship. Tom tried to crawl after him with his arm extended and stumbled to a stop. He knew it was their destiny.

They were sucked into the vortex's opening on a ripple's edge. Their 21st-century memories faded into a familiar gray soundscape jingled. It dissipated into the sunlight that broke through the clouds as a fiery rainbow stretched across the ocean.

A seagull screeched with its meal clung in its talons. It landed on the rock where they had once stood. They were transported out of this time to another dimension of themselves.

Days later, the local police connected the abandoned vehicle with a missing persons report.

Theresa, Sally, and Margie were heartbroken with their losses.

They remained close friends.

～～～

Goddess Iris had regained all her celestial powers as ripples continue to spread long after the stone is gone. Each ripple is much like the last, but as time passes, each ripple is smaller than the last, fainter. The surface of the water smooths over in time, but a discerning eye can still find signs of the disturbance long after the stone has settled to the bottom.

The Freds, the Basters and the Irenes of this world are all reflections of each other, and of the three deities who briefly touched this world: Zephyr, Bastet and myself. When we departed back into no-space, some of our energy remained, and we left newly forming ripples in our wake. The Toms, the Pearls: they are of this world, not deities, but their love nevertheless resonates across time.

And, in one ripple, a wish on the amulet came true.

The poet William Blake wrote of seeing the world in a grain of sand, and Heaven in a wildflower. If you know where to look, you can also find living memories of timeless beings on the surface of a pond.

- CHAPTER 20 -

Manhattan and Toronto 2164

Interstellar sounds whistle in the year 2164, ushering in the last stars into its zig-zag alignment for the Age of Aquarius reign. This calculated move replaced the Age of Pisces: the retiring constellation ruler. The Zodiac wheel positioned the constellation Aquarius: the water-bearer star sign. It'll rule over this planet for the next two thousand years.

It was a late summer afternoon in New York. Steamy hot with wispy cloud strands etched into the blue sky. The world has become ecologically conscious. The day's most popular entertainments are the live-streaming virtual reality tours of the changing colors of the foliage in the nature reserves of the northern hemisphere, and goose-eye views of the fall migration.

Practical small-scale fusion generators provide nearly limitless power, and genetically engineered tar-eating bacteria are slowly cleaning up the toxic waste from the era of petroleum.

For the wealthy, trips to the Langrange points in Earth orbit were popular, and sought after resort destinations on the Moon and Mars outshone the cruise ship industry long ago. Though, submarine-style vessels still criss-cross the oceans for the benefit of the adventure class that needs the physical stimulation of earthbound travel, however primitive it is.

Lunar and Martian prospectors were constantly discovering, exploiting, and making small fortunes from shallowly buried ice deposits to supply water and air to the growing colonies. The Earth-Moon race is on the verge of becoming an official Olympic sport.

Theresa was a thirty something year old clothing designer, based in Manhattan, but with outlets on all three worlds. Her 3-D printed creations using recycled materials are for the wealthy rocketing traveler. She is one of the top style-definers for the worldly trendsetter for the fashion and resort industry.

A series of beeps, bops and bleeping tiny colored flashes appear on a translucent oval screen atop a pedestal. Theresa is lying on a recliner bed in a modern living pod fully equipped for comfort. Device-generated mirrors were beamed along the walls to contain her memory recalls, from rippling out of the present time sequence before the image captures were interpreted.

Theresa is finishing a breakthrough session with her doctor. He was a world-renowned hypnosis specialist in Toronto. She was time traveling into her past lives, with the hope of changing her present situation.

"One, two, three ... stay with me, breathe." The doctor intones, along with quick finger snaps. Theresa's eyelashes flutter gently. She presses a purple button on the hydraulic chair as her body rises into an upright pose. Her dark hair swirls up into stacked curls, held with a stylish glittering bow of her own design. Her holo-display is currently slaved to the doctor's display. He has switched it so instead of her dreams, they are now looking at each other. But he has left one image from her session, shimmering in the air between them.

"Looks like we've made some real progress. But, that is judging from the fleeting images. You will need to tell me about what you saw, and what you felt. As you know, I can only see the visuals from your past lives, and it is their lingering, emotional energy that really matters."

"What a journey. It felt like it was real."

"History is real and it's always present if it declares itself to you." This image captured from her dream intrigues him. He looks closer at the man.

"I lived a life as a woman named Pearl, maybe even an Irene, Alene? I felt the names all meant Pearl."

"Go on."

"Pearl waited a lifetime, actually many of them, for her love to return forevermore. Thomas? But she also called him Tom. They both believed in fate. He made sure they would never be apart again."

"Tom?" His fingers tapped the desk, nervously.

"How did Pearl look?"

"She has golden-brown eyes and wore a dress."

~~~~~~

"Tell me about Tom."

"He was a blue-eyed sailor, and a captain. He was also a businessman, and a gambler. Oh, and he was undying romantic from what I recall. Is it possible he was all of those?"

"With past life regression, you can see multiple lives at the same time. It can be hard to sort them out, and often not always necessary to do so."

"Two or maybe more Toms then. But they all vanish in storms, or thunderclaps."

"Hmm, interesting. A past life can also be part of someone else's that has rippled into your own experiences. Sometimes, one's fate may be to fulfill another person's purpose for a future outcome, as their fated destiny was unfulfilled. Or, delayed somehow due to unpredictable detours on their life journey."

"Oh."

"Freewill plays a big role in it, but that's a discussion for another time."

"I see, a shared life experience for a future outcome."

"Exactly! You're progressing fine. Good work."

Theresa sits up and looks into the screen. "What's that behind you?"

"That?" He swivels his chair to look at the wall behind him. Theresa stares at the portrait. She has seen that richly gilded frame in her hypnosis-induced trance. "I recently inherited it from a long lost relative whom

I never heard of, from the eastern shores of Canada. Interesting isn't it?" He questioned himself silently.

He wondered whether he had lost his family gift that was inherited from his great grandfather. But why hadn't he noticed the subtle nuances in the images of her man. Precision eyesight of an eagle was passed down every other generation. It was what made him successful in reading holo-displays with accuracy.

Theresa swirls her fingers in the air to enlarge the captain's image and the woman held lovingly in his arms. She could feel their happiness by the look on their faces. Then a realization hit her.

"That's Pearl! That was one of my former lives, or a life I stepped into. I was her, reading a book or a letter or something, in an old attic. There was also a portrait. That's the same painting, but without the woman."

"So, the portrait was only of a sea captain?" He was trying to understand.

"Yes, but otherwise it's exactly the same in that gilt frame. It's absolutely identical with the position of the brass plaque. There's no doubt in my mind, but...." Theresa studies the couple's faces in her doctor's office.

"But, what?"

"Except he looks happy in your portrait."

"Do you remember anything else?"

"It was in the next set of rolling pictures."

"Go on."

"I was ... I mean Pearl entered the room and walked over to the portrait, beside a scrunched up cloth on the floor. Then, there was a thunderclap and Pearl vanished."

"Oh?"

"I saw someone in shiny boots and a jacket with brass buttons. Some kind of officer came into the room."

"Year?"

"1925."

"That's a long time ago."

"Oh, it was in Toronto where you are, on a street called ... Jarvis."

"There is a street in Toronto called Jarvis. It is part of the Heritage Conservation District."

A soft gong reverberates over the VR connection.

"Looks like we're out of time. Your account has been charged and the receipt sent. Our next scheduled virtual reality session is on your calendar. You're progressing fine. You should recover from your concussion soon, according to your micro-gamma scans, but your eardrum and ankle will take time.

You'll be ready to return to your regular work schedule by the next equinox. Hopefully after this session, you'll no longer be an accident-prone you. I believe you may have just cleared the magnetized mind-pattern in your subconscious that attracts these situations."

"Thank you doctor."

～～～～

Dr. Adler was drawn to the plaque at the bottom of the portrait's frame that hung on his wall. It was dated 1835. He looked closely at the painting. The brushstrokes used to paint the woman overlap the man. She was added later on. Disappointed, he realized it's not a priceless antique after all.

He turned around to look out the window at the rolling waves on Lake Ontario, and its mysterious vastness. Clouds scud across the sky, streaks of gray marking falling rain in the distance. A rainbow is forming over the lake.

A gentle ringtone draws the doctor's attention. He moves his finger over the button, as his best friend comes into focus on a floating screen before him.

"An opportunity like this doesn't orbit around often. You owe me a favor."

"You're right, go on."

"My sister Margie's friend, the lonely one."

"I'm enjoying my Toronto hotel pod alone. I'm officially unattached, and plan to stay that way. It took a lot of work to get to this point."

"You promised, my friend. You might have a lot in common. I know a jazzy cybercafé along the walking path to the Toronto Islands. It just opened after being boarded-up for well over a century. The land couldn't be altered or sold due to an old city title issue. It had to remain as a free-standing public establishment."

"Sounds intriguing."

"The proprietor kept its antique log cabin charm, super-retro, with live celestial-sound music and glassed-in sitting pods. Wait till you taste their berry-spice muffins made on the premise. The recipe was supposedly from a 21st-century storeowner. It was written on a piece of paper wedged under a floorboard behind a library counter from an earlier era, that has carved initials in the wood, with a heart-shape outline."

"Who hasn't heard about it, it's all over the solar-network satellites. Hmm, actual writing paper. What a find for a treasure hunter! The proprietor felt nostalgic about the place and has begun to research its history. Folklore says it's haunted ever since its doors were closed in 2023. Apparently the owner vanished overnight during a storm on Lake Ontario."

Tom gave a sigh of resignation, tinged with something approaching interest. Fred waited patiently, he knew his friend was almost there.

"OK, Fred. I'll do it."

"I've just sent you her contact credentials, call her."

"Got it, and what's her name?"

"Iris Montgomery, she's out of this world."

"Really?" Tom steps toward the portrait of the captain and his woman, and brushes his finger lightly on her face.

"Did I mention she has a cat?"

Rainbows swirl, as sunlight glistens off the ocean waves. Goddess Iris pours from her water pitcher, and the flow of time on Earth responds, ripples spreading ever outwards, intersecting, waxing and waning, reflecting our fates, which cannot be escaped.

ABOUT THE AUTHOR

Toronto born, I grew up fascinated by rainbows, as my mother would remind me of a childhood fire rainbow that my sister and I witnessed in the late sixties. Yes! This phenomena was rare, but does exist. Its awe-inspiring colors still come to mind. It was only upon completion of this book that it dawned on me: I was indeed on a hero's journey into the exploration of color and light from a young age, and this being a piece of the puzzle.

In 1996, I had a vision and my company, Spectrahue, was born and soon developed a color therapy system for the spiritual seeker, and metaphysical practitioner.

The writing of *Ripples* began in late autumn, 2019. It was inspired by a dream vision and I was on it. Its prose rippled throughout the COVID pandemic with the backdrop of chaos from construction that's changing Toronto's landscape.

I feel a small ripple sweep past my window. A squirrel scurries about for a peanut I had tossed its way, as I write these last words about me.

—Julianne Bien